the Chibineko Kitchen

First published in Great Britain in 2024 by John Murray (Publishers)

Original Japanese edition published in 2020 by Kobunsha Co. Ltd., Tokyo
Chibinekotei No Omoidegohan: Kuroneko to Hatsukoi Sandwich

1

A CIP catalogue record for this title is available from the British Library

Paperback ISBN 9781399817615
ebook ISBN 9781399817646

Typeset in Baskerville MT by Hewer Text UK Ltd, Edinburgh
Printed and bound in Great Britain by Clays Ltd, Elcograf S.p.A.

John Murray policy is to use papers that are natural, renewable and recyclable products and made from wood grown in sustainable forests. The logging and manufacturing processes are expected to conform to the environmental regulations of the country of origin.

Carmelite House
50 Victoria Embankment
London EC4Y 0DZ

www.johnmurraypress.co.uk

John Murray Press, part of Hodder & Stoughton Limited
An Hachette UK company

The authorised representative in the EEA is
Hachette Ireland, 8 Castlecourt Centre,
Castleknock Road, Castleknock, Dublin 15, D15 YF6A, Ireland

the Chibineko Kitchen

YUTA TAKAHASHI

Translated by

CAT ANDERSON

JOHN MURRAY

1

A ginger-patch cat and a dish of simmered fish

アイナメ

Fat greenling

A delicacy, fat greenling can be fished in the waters all around Japan, by rocky shores or out on reefs where its food is plentiful. It can be caught off Uchibo, on the western side of the Boso Peninsula in Chiba Prefecture. The fishing season runs from summer to winter.

Fat greenling has a mild flavour and is delicious served as sashimi with the skin seared; marinated and grilled with sansho pepper leaf; or cooked in a hotpot.

The black-tailed gulls were soaring.

She had come across them before in books and on TV, but this was probably her first time seeing them in real life. They were known as 'sea cats', and with their mewing cries – *miaoow, miaoow* – it was obvious why. There was something mournful about the sound, and it put her in mind of a stray kitten.

Kotoko Niki, who was turning twenty that year, was visiting a seaside town in Uchibo. Blue sea, blue sky, a sandy beach – and running along behind it, an unpaved path covered in white shells instead of tarmac. According to the directions she'd been given over the phone, if she continued walking along this path she would reach the Chibineko Kitchen. That was the name of her destination: the restaurant by the sea.

It wasn't even nine in the morning yet, which was perhaps why there was no one out on the beach. In fact, she had hardly caught a glimpse of anyone on her way here. This seemed to be a quiet town, unlike Tokyo where she'd come from today.

'A town by the sea . . .' she murmured. She gazed at the gulls and the beach a little longer, and then set off down the white path. The seashells clattered noisily under her feet; she felt as though she was disturbing the atmosphere of the sleepy town with her racket.

It was the middle of October but autumn still hadn't arrived. The summer weather continued unabated, the sun beating down incessantly from a cloudless blue sky. Kotoko was glad she'd worn a hat with a wide brim to protect her from the sunshine. The hat was white and she wore a white dress too. With her fair skin, long hair and her neat, almost old-fashioned clothes, she would have fitted in well in a previous century. Her older brother Yuito had loved to tease her about this. 'You look so retro, Kotoko,' he would say, 'like a posh young lady from the fifties.' Even just remembering it, she had to fight back the tears.

It wasn't out of frustration at having been teased. The reason Kotoko felt like crying was because her brother was no longer with her. He was no longer part of this world, having died three months earlier.

He had died, and it was Kotoko's fault.

The universities were off for the summer holidays. It was evening, and Kotoko was on her way out. An author she was keen on had just written a new book, and she planned to pick up a copy from the big bookshop in front of the station. She could easily have bought it online but it would be sad, she thought, if any more bookshops went out of business.

Arriving at the shop, she found they had stacks of the title she was after – it looked as though it was selling well. She bought a copy and left.

It was after six, and Kotoko remembered being dazzled by the evening sun, low in the sky. She'd squinted, her gaze landing on the station for no particular reason when out walked her brother.

'Hey, Yuito,' she called over to him. 'Oh, hi, Kotoko,' he replied. It was a chance meeting but both station and bookshop were in their neighbourhood, not even ten minutes' walk from home. If either of them went out, they'd usually think of heading home around now in order to make it back in time for dinner, so bumping into him wasn't such an unusual coincidence.

'Heading back?'

'Yes.'

They didn't talk on the way but just walked along in silence. When they were together they didn't feel the need to make conversation.

Kotoko's mind was on the book she'd just bought: she was looking forward to getting home and starting it. She didn't have the faintest suspicion that anything other than a peaceful evening awaited. Her brother's presence hardly even registered with her.

When they'd been walking for five minutes, they stopped at the traffic lights. It was a narrow crossroads leading to the station and it was always busy. Kotoko had felt no sense of foreboding; she'd just stood there waiting. She hadn't looked at her brother. She didn't know what expression he'd had on his face as they waited for the lights.

They had only been standing there for a moment when the lights changed. Kotoko stepped off the kerb, without a glance at Yuito. They were more than half-way across the road when it happened. She heard the noise of an engine close by – too close – and she looked round sharply. A car was racing towards them, towards Kotoko, at furious speed.

It's going to hit me!

She sensed the danger but her body froze and she couldn't run. She was petrified, her legs paralysed by fear. She almost squeezed her eyes shut in terror.

Then suddenly she felt a thump on her back. For an instant she thought the car had hit her, but the impact had come from another direction. Someone had sent her flying.

Kotoko tumbled onto the far pavement. She had scraped her knees and banged her elbows but the car had missed her.

What happened?

She wished she didn't know; that she'd remained ignorant of the facts. But there was a moment when Kotoko had looked back. She should have closed her eyes, but she hadn't, and she'd seen it all. It was her brother who had pushed her out of the way, who had saved her: just as the car had been about to hit her, he had given her a powerful shove.

'Why?' Kotoko murmured, but no one heard her.

She was safe, but her brother had been sent flying as the car sped over the crossing. He had landed like a puppet with its strings cut and was no longer moving; he was lying motionless in the road, in an unnatural, twisted pose.

A car horn beeped and someone screamed. Voices flew back and forth.

'Call an ambulance!'

'Call the police!'

'Hey, are you all right?'

The question must have been directed at her. She was aware of it but was unable to reply. She couldn't think properly and her voice wouldn't come out. She just gazed at the now unmoving body of her brother. She had a feeling she might have whispered his name.

She heard the ambulance and the police sirens but by the time the medics arrived, Yuito was dead.

Kotoko walked along the seashell path. She was unable to hold back her tears and the scene blurred before her.

She had cried every day since her brother died, but she couldn't do so in a place like this. She was supposed to be going to a restaurant and it would be embarrassing if she arrived all weepy, and her eyes puffy. She stopped still and looked up at the heavens, fighting back the tears. Gazing at the sky and its never-ending blueness, she felt as though it would absorb her.

Feeling a little calmer now, Kotoko looked at her watch – it was almost the time of her booking. She had better hurry to the Chibineko Kitchen.

She was just setting off when it happened. Suddenly, a gust came in off the sea. The weather had been so calm, she was unprepared for the strength of the wind which lifted her hat off her head and carried it away.

'Oh, no!' The hat soared towards the water. At this rate it was going to end up in the sea.

Kotoko had to either chase after her errant hat or abandon it. But she liked that hat; she wasn't prepared to let it go. She had never been much of a runner but she dashed off in pursuit.

And then a figure appeared, sprinting past her. A man. *He's trying to catch my hat for me.*

From behind, the person who had overtaken her looked exactly like her dead brother. He was tall and slender, and there was that slightly long hair she remembered.

'Yuito!' she murmured in shock, but perhaps he couldn't hear. He didn't turn round, but instead leapt towards the sun.

He looked beautiful, flying through the air with the light behind him – almost as though he had sprouted wings, like an angel. Kotoko thought her brother had come back to her from the other world; perhaps she was witnessing a miracle.

She'd come here thinking only of Yuito and wanting to see him. She'd come here hoping for something extraordinary, and if this was it, nothing could make her happier.

But it wasn't to be. Kotoko soon realised that no miracle had occurred.

The man caught the hat, grasping it in his right hand just as it seemed about to sail out over the water. He turned round and Kotoko saw his face clearly. He looked roughly the same age as her brother – in his early twenties – but it wasn't Yuito. And there was something about him that made 'young man', or even 'boy', seem more fitting than 'man'. Kotoko's brother had been strongly masculine in appearance and he wore a suntan well, but this young man's face was softer. His skin was so pale it was almost colourless, and his glasses were elegant and thin-rimmed.

Are those women's glasses? Kotoko wondered. They certainly looked like it, yet they suited the young man's androgynous features. He resembled the main character in a girls' manga: his was the face of the tender hero who captures the heroine's heart.

The young man came up beside Kotoko and held out the hat. 'Here you go.'

His voice was as gentle as his looks. Kotoko felt as though she'd heard it before somewhere, but she couldn't place it.

'Thank you very much,' she said, flustered. Taking the hat from him, she bowed. He'd gone to all that trouble to chase it for her while she'd just stood there gawping, remembering her brother. Where had he come from anyway? Kotoko had thought she was the only person around.

'You must be Ms Kotoko Niki,' he said.

Kotoko had never met him before, yet he knew her name. She nodded in surprise.

'I . . . Yes, I am . . . And you are . . .?' she asked tentatively.

'My apologies for not introducing myself sooner. I'm Kai Fukuchi – from the Chibineko Kitchen. Thank you very much for making a reservation with us today.' He bowed low as he gave his name. Kotoko was polite, but this young man's manners were on a whole different level.

Kai, with the elegant spectacles that suited him so well, was from the restaurant where Kotoko was heading. Yes, that was where she'd heard his voice – he had taken her booking over the phone.

After Yuito's funeral, it was as though a light had been extinguished in Kotoko's house. Nobody talked any more.

Kotoko's father was employed by a small local credit union and her mother worked part time at the supermarket. They were both quiet, mild-mannered people. 'Your parents are so nice, Kotoko,' was what friends always said when they came over. And it was true, her parents were nice. She'd never once heard them raise their voices.

Her brother had been her parents' pride and joy. At primary school he was already excelling in class and he was sporty, too. In junior high school he was head of the pupil council. And, as though it was pre-ordained, he got into the best state senior high school in the area, and then passed his university entrance exams and was accepted to study law at a prestigious and notoriously selective private university. His life was plain sailing.

Kotoko had assumed that when Yuito graduated he'd go on to become a lawyer, maybe even a prosecutor. But before Yuito had completed his first year he told his family he was dropping out. Kotoko was surprised, but not as shocked as her parents.

'What do you mean, dropping out?' their father asked, as though cross-examining Yuito.

'But what will you do?' said their mother.

Their parents' faces were taut with concern, their opposition to the idea evident in their voices. Nevertheless, Kotoko's brother had looked them straight in the eye.

'I want to be an actor,' he said.

On starting university, Yuito had joined a small local theatre company. Kotoko knew he was serious about it, but she'd never imagined he'd announce that he was quitting university. The thought didn't seem to have occurred to her parents either.

'Can't you carry on with your acting alongside your studies?' they asked. It was a fair question. What parents would want to let their child drop out of a prestigious university – one that he'd done so well to get into in the first place – just like that?

'I don't want to do it in my spare time, I want to give it everything I've got.' Yuito's reply was unambiguous. He had already made up his mind, that much was clearly written on his face. He was going to become an actor.

'Isn't it very difficult, though?' This was another fair question, from their mother. Kotoko didn't know much about acting but surely, she thought, only a handful of people actually succeeded. Staying on at university and then going on to some law-related job after graduation was definitely the more sensible option. But her brother didn't back down.

'I know it's a tough industry. But I want to give it a shot,' he said, without a shred of doubt in his voice. He was probably already envisaging the road ahead. 'I've only got one life and I don't want to have any regrets,' he said so forcefully that their parents were almost persuaded. 'I'll have something to show for it in three years,' Yuito told them. 'I'll get a part in a TV show, you'll see. And if my acting career doesn't take off, I'll apply for a place at a national university and go into the civil service.'

At this, their parents agreed. They probably thought there was no point arguing with Yuito when he was so set on it. Maybe they believed he'd end up a civil servant. If Kotoko was being honest, so did she. Becoming an actor, getting on TV – it sounded like a fantasy.

But before the three years were up, her brother was making good on his ambitions. The year Kotoko got into university he was picked for a leading stage role, and then the following year he got through multiple auditions for a TV series and won a major part as the best friend of the protagonist.

He was attracting notice, being featured in weekly magazines as an up-and-coming actor and even appearing in TV interviews. 'That's quite something,' their father had said. Each time Yuito appeared in a magazine, their mother would cut out the article. Kotoko's parents were waiting eagerly for the TV series to air. Kotoko was proud of her brother too – 'Yuito, that's amazing!' she said to him. She knew how hard he had worked. He'd poured his blood, sweat and tears into his acting career. Kotoko had gone along to rehearsals at his theatre company a number of times and knew he had many admirers there. Talent had undoubtedly played a part but – more importantly – he trained harder than anyone else. She knew he often went out to do vocal exercises in the local park.

I've only got one life and I don't want to have any regrets.

That was what her brother liked to say. But he'd died before he could achieve his dream.

Life continued. But their family of four had become three. If her brother hadn't saved her, Kotoko would be dead – but Yuito would be alive. Kotoko wished he hadn't sacrificed his own life for the sake of hers. It wasn't as though she had wanted to die, but she didn't want to be living in place of her brother.

Kotoko was interested in the theatre herself and she had loved seeing Yuito's company perform. The little troupe was always short of actors, and one night when they needed someone to take on a bit part, the company's director, Kumagai, asked her to be in the play.

'Kuma' means 'bear' and, true to his name, Kumagai was a big, bear-like man. He was bearded and looked as though he could be in his forties or fifties, but in fact he was only about ten years older than Yuito. Kumagai had founded the theatre company, and it was also he who'd spotted Yuito's talent. He had the kind of fierce look that would make young trouble-makers on the street scarper, but his eyes were kind and he had a warm, friendly smile. Maybe the reason Kotoko had agreed to get up on stage, despite her shyness, was because it was Kumagai who was in charge. He had a quality that drew people to him.

After her second performance, Kumagai said to her: 'You can act, Kotoko.'

'Oh, come on.' She thought Kumagai was teasing her. All she'd done was walk on and off; she didn't even speak.

But he looked deadly serious. 'Kotoko, when you're on stage the place lights up. Even when you don't have any lines.'

It was the first time anyone had ever said anything like that to her. She had been a reserved child, always tucked away in the corner of the classroom. She wasn't like her popular brother, anyone who knew Kotoko knew that. And yet Kumagai wouldn't stop praising her.

'You've got more stage presence than Yuito, you know.' Surely this had to be a joke, but he said it with a straight face. What was more, there was someone else who agreed.

'Yeah, he's right.'

Her brother had been quietly listening in, and now he was nodding. 'I might have been playing the lead, but everyone was looking at you, Kotoko.'

'Are you sure it's not because I was rubbish?'

'Nope, it's because they really liked you. You're a natural, you steal the show even just playing a bit part.'

'Stop making fun of me,' Kotoko objected. Her brother shrugged and raised his eyebrows. She thought about protesting further, but then Kumagai interjected.

'Why don't you give acting a proper go? I reckon you could outshine your brother.'

'No way,' Kotoko said, trying to get out of it. She had enjoyed being on stage but she was sure she had zero talent. She was content being the icing on the cake that was her brother. Non-speaking roles were right up her street. Anyway, she only turned up at the theatre company because Yuito was there.

So when he died, she stopped going to the group. She decided to take a break from university too. She didn't want to do anything or go anywhere; she just stayed in her room. When she did go out, it was only to visit her brother's grave.

It was something Kumagai had said that had brought Kotoko to the seaside town.

Kumagai wasn't just the director of Yuito's theatre company; he and Yuito had also been good friends. On days off, they went on motorcycling trips together and fished along the rocky coastline. It wasn't unusual for them to go quite far afield.

When Kotoko saw Kumagai again, it was in the cemetery where her brother lay. She had gone to visit the family grave and found him standing there, his head bowed and palms pressed together. She didn't feel like speaking to him, but it would have been rude to run away and anyway, she didn't have the energy. As she approached the grave, Kumagai looked up.

'Oh, hello. I haven't seen you for ages.'

'Thank you very much for your recent support,' Kotoko said, trying to get away with a stock greeting, but Kumagai wouldn't be deterred.

'Are you eating properly?' he asked. He must have noticed her gaunt cheeks. Kotoko hadn't had any appetite for ages. She tried to force herself to eat so she didn't keel over, but sometimes it slipped her mind. On this particular day she hadn't eaten anything at all, but she didn't plan on admitting it.

'Yes, I'm eating,' she replied. Kumagai said nothing; he could probably tell it was a lie. He just looked at Kotoko with concern. She shifted her gaze to the Niki family grave, avoiding Kumagai's eyes. The gravestone was clean: her parents must have been looking after it. It was old and worn – they'd had it for generations, after all – but it had been polished until there wasn't a speck of dirt on it. An image appeared in her mind of her mother and father taking dust cloths to the stone.

Kotoko thought about her parents. Maybe they'd cried as they cleaned the gravestone. Cried for their dead son, their pride and joy. *You should never have saved me*, she wanted to mutter at the stone. It was so hopelessly painful being the one who survived. Her eyes pricked, and she was attempting to hold back her tears when Kumagai's voice reached her.

'Have you heard of the Chibineko Kitchen?'

Kotoko was bewildered by this abrupt question, and the urge to cry receded. 'Is it a restaurant or something?' she asked, wondering what on earth Kumagai was talking about.

'Kind of, or a cafe, I suppose. It's this little place by the sea in Uchibo, in Chiba. You don't know it?'

Kotoko had never heard the name before. In fact she hardly ever went to Chiba Prefecture despite it being close to Tokyo. Even when her brother was alive she went just once or twice a year with him, and then only to visit Disneyland. She certainly had no memory of ever going to a restaurant there.

Kotoko shook her head.

'When I went fishing with Yuito, we ate there a few times,' Kumagai explained. 'The place is run by this beautiful lady, she's around fifty . . .' He broke off. Then he said, 'She'll make you a remembrance meal.'

This was new to Kotoko, too. A remembrance meal? As she was puzzling over the unfamiliar words, Kumagai spoke again.

'Kagezen. You know?'

Kotoko had heard of that. When someone was away from home for a long time, their family would make food offerings called kagezen to pray for their safe return. And it was also sometimes what you called the food offered up to the deceased at Buddhist funeral services. She assumed Kumagai was referring to the latter. When Yuito died, her family had offered up kagezen alongside the food provided for guests attending the wake and after the cremation.

'When you eat a remembrance meal at the Chibineko Kitchen, you can hear your loved one's voice again. Their memory comes back to you,' said Kumagai.

'Oh, right,' Kotoko murmured to show she was listening. But she couldn't follow what Kumagai was trying to say.

'I mean, someone who's dead,' he said.

'What?'

'And they say that sometimes the person even visits you.'

The dead person visits you?

'Do you understand what I mean?' Kumagai asked her. Kotoko shook her head; of course not. 'If you go to the Chibineko Kitchen, you might be able to talk to Yuito. That's what I'm saying.'

Surely it had to be a bad joke. What Kumagai was telling her was absurd. But his expression was seriousness itself. He didn't look as though he was lying. And he had been her brother's mentor on the stage as well as a close friend despite their age difference. At both the wake and the funeral, Kumagai had wept more than anyone else.

He's telling the truth. It was impossible yet Kotoko believed Kumagai's words – she wanted to believe them.

'I might really see my brother?' she queried, making doubly sure she had understood.

'I don't know. I'm just saying maybe,' Kumagai replied. Well, maybe was good enough. All other thoughts were driven out of her head.

'Please, will you tell me more about the Chibineko Kitchen?'

'Hello, this is the Chibineko Kitchen.' A young man answered when Kotoko rang the number Kumagai had given her.

'I'd like to make a booking,' she said.

'Certainly. The restaurant closes at ten o'clock in the morning. Please may I confirm that will be all right?'

'In the morning?'

'That's correct. We're open until 10 a.m.'

'Oh . . . All right. That's fine.' Maybe the Chibineko Kitchen only did breakfast. Kotoko couldn't quite see why a place like that would be providing kagezen but, of course, the restaurant was free to serve whatever they liked.

'Very good,' came the response. What a polite way of speaking – his manners were almost old-fashioned. The man's soft, gentle voice soothed Kotoko and she found she could talk to him without getting nervous.

'Could I please order a remembrance meal?' she asked.

'Certainly.'

With this short exchange, the restaurant accepted her booking. Kotoko had just given her name and number when, as though he had forgotten to mention something important, the man said, 'We have a cat in the restaurant. May I confirm that won't be an issue for you?'

The place was called the Chibineko Kitchen – 'chibi-neko' meaning 'little cat' – so it was hardly surprising. Kotoko didn't mind cats: 'Yes, that's fine.'

'Excellent.'

She could picture whoever was on the other end of the line bowing his head. His sincerity seemed to be transmitted down the phone to her, and she felt herself warm to him.

'Thank you very much for your booking. We look forward to seeing you,' he said, courteous to the last.

Kumagai told Kotoko how to get to the Chibineko Kitchen. If she caught the rapid line from Tokyo station, she'd be there in an hour and a half; it was close enough that she could return the same day.

'Say hello to Nanami and Chibi for me,' Kumagai had said. Nanami was apparently the name of the restaurant's owner, and Chibi was the cat.

'I will,' Kotoko promised, but she'd forgotten almost immediately. She didn't mean to disappoint Kumagai, but the thought that she might soon see her brother again pushed everything else out of her mind.

So she boarded the train and travelled to the town by the sea. As the Chibineko Kitchen was some distance from the station, Kotoko caught a bus where she sat, swaying from side to side for a quarter of an hour or so, before getting out and walking along the bank of the Koitogawa River. Then she came to the white seashell path where she encountered Kai Fukuchi who retrieved her flyaway hat.

Kai was wearing a long-sleeved shirt and black trousers. His dark hair, a little on the long side, was being ruffled by the sea breeze.

'Allow me to show you to the restaurant.'

'Thank you,' Kotoko said, and they set off. He hardly needed to show her the way: they'd only been walking for a few minutes when the restaurant came into view.

It was a wooden building with blue walls which reminded Kotoko of a boathouse or an elegant beach hut. It was roomy and had two storeys – perhaps the owner lived there, too. There was no sign on the building but beside the door was a chalkboard – the A-frame, free-standing kind you often see outside cafes and restaurants. On the board was written in white lettering:

The Chibineko Kitchen
We serve remembrance meals.

And below that, there was a little note:

This restaurant has a cat.

This was embellished with an illustration of a kitten. The letters and the picture, drawn with soft, round strokes, suggested to Kotoko that it was a woman's hand. She couldn't see a menu anywhere, and there was no mention of the fact that the restaurant was only open for breakfast. It didn't seem as though the place was raring to pull customers in.

While Kotoko was puzzling over the chalkboard, she heard a sound coming from behind it – a mewing.

'*Miaow.*'

She peered round the board and saw a tiny cat sitting there – an adorable thing, white with ginger patches. Cats were a fixture in any seaside town but still Kotoko was surprised to see quite such a small creature out in front of the restaurant. Was it a stray? If so, it didn't seem very afraid of people and its fur was beautiful. She gazed at the kitten, enchanted.

'Now, please remember I've told you not to go outside,' she heard Kai say. This remark was directed at the kitten, but he had spoken just as he would to another person. *He's polite even when he's talking to a cat! He doesn't just put it on for the customers.*

'I would like you to stay inside. Do you understand?' he asked, shooting a very stern glance at the kitten before turning back to Kotoko almost deferentially. 'We seem to be going about things in the wrong order this morning, but never mind. Please allow me to introduce you to the family cat, Chibi.'

What an excessively courteous way to introduce a kitten.

'*Miaow*.' The tiny cat – Chibi – mewed as though in greeting. So this was the restaurant's mascot.

'He'll be back outside before long,' Kai said, by way of explanation. It seemed that the mischievous Chibi was something of an escape artist. 'All right, please make your way inside,' Kai said to the kitten, who replied to this command with a short '*Miaow*'. Not only that, he actually turned and trotted off towards the restaurant door, waving his tail nimbly from side to side as though beckoning Kotoko and Kai to follow. Kai overtook the little kitten and opened the door. This time he addressed Kotoko.

'Welcome to the Chibineko Kitchen. Please, come in.'

It was a small restaurant with only eight seats and was spotlessly clean. There was no counter, just two round tables with four chairs apiece. The furniture was wooden and the place was suffused with the cosy atmosphere of a log cabin. In one corner stood a tall, antique-looking grandfather clock which was still in working order, and was marking time with a loud *tick-tock, tick-tock*.

A large window in one wall looked out to the sea off Uchibo where the black-tailed gulls soared through the skies above the blue water, crying '*miaoow, miaoow*'.

'*Miaow*,' Chibi mewed towards the window, as if in response. Then, seeming to lose interest in the gulls he wandered off in the direction of the old clock. Kotoko was watching Chibi when Kai said, 'Will this one be all right for you?' He was indicating a seat by the window where Kotoko would have a good view of the sea.

'Yes, thank you,' she said, and Kai pulled out the chair for her.

Next to the grandfather clock was a wooden rocking chair. By this time the kitten had curled itself up on the chair, closed its eyes and fallen fast asleep. It was a picture of tranquillity.

You can hear your loved one's voice again . . . Sometimes the person even visits you.

That was what Kumagai had said – but the restaurant wasn't what Kotoko had imagined. And she couldn't see any sign of Nanami, the lady in her fifties who was supposed to cook the food. She was thinking about asking after her when, as though to get things moving, Kai spoke to her again.

'Now, if you don't mind waiting for a few minutes, we will prepare your remembrance meal.'

Kotoko had left the house about three hours earlier, while dawn was still breaking. She had needed to catch the first train of the day to make it to the restaurant on time.

Despite the early hour, the light was on in the butsuma – the room where the family kept their butsudan, the Buddhist altar where they remembered Yuito. Her mother and father were awake: it wasn't just Kotoko who'd been counting the sleepless nights.

The butsuma was separated from the hallway by a sliding paper door. Kotoko could see the shadows of her parents on the other side, but she didn't say anything to tell them she was going out. When she imagined how they must be feeling, she couldn't bring herself to speak.

Despite her parents' initial objections to Yuito's change of career, soon they were caught up in the excitement of his journey. They'd eagerly anticipated his TV debut: Yuito's hopes had been their hopes too. And they had been extinguished. Her brother was dead, and her parents had become like ghosts, crushed by grief. They were always shut away in the butsuma.

I should have been the one to die.

Kotoko's mind always led her back to this thought. Even now, at the Chibineko Kitchen, she couldn't dismiss it. It wasn't just because her brother had died to save her. It was because – Kotoko believed – if Yuito had survived instead of her, their parents probably wouldn't have fallen into such a deep depression. And even if they had, she was sure Yuito would have managed to pull them out of it, whereas Kotoko could barely even speak to them.

Her thoughts tormented her. *I'm the one who survived. The useless one. Me, with my total lack of purpose.* She didn't know how to go on living. She was lost, she was on the verge of tears – and then she heard a mew from down by her feet.

It was Chibi. He must have woken up from his snooze on the rocking chair, and now he was on the floor, peering up at her. He almost looked worried, and his expression was so funny that Kotoko suddenly found herself wanting to laugh. The moment passed and she had managed not to cry.

'Thanks,' she said to the little cat, and then Kai appeared from the kitchen. He was wearing a charming apron made of white denim with a kitten embroidered on the chest – Chibi, maybe. He came over to the table.

'I apologise for keeping you waiting,' he said. He had brought out the food on a lacquered tray: rice, miso soup and fish simmered in soy sauce. He set out the dishes on the table. Everything looked freshly cooked and was steaming hot. Chibi mewed, clearly enticed by the smell of the fish. He sounded as though he wanted some, but Kotoko didn't spare him a glance. Her gaze was fixed on the dish of simmered fish herself. She couldn't believe it.

'Fat greenling,' she found herself murmuring.

This was her brother's remembrance meal.

Fat greenling, a long, spindle-shaped rockfish which inhabits the rocky reefs around the coast, is well known for its delicious flavour, but you don't often come across it in Tokyo's supermarkets, or on the table of the average household. It's not cheap either, but something of a luxury.

Kotoko had never heard of it until her brother introduced it to her. When Yuito went fishing with Kumagai, now and then he would bring home a fat greenling.

'I'm thinking of becoming a professional angler,' Kotoko remembered her brother boasting, half-joking. Yuito was good at whatever he tried his hand at. He didn't leave the cooking to their mother either, but prepared the catch himself.

Kotoko had an interest in cooking and she often watched as her brother gutted and prepared the fish. Yuito never treated her as a nuisance but instead talked to her while he worked.

'Ideally I'd like to serve it as namero . . .' he said as if recalling the flavour. Namero was a local speciality from Chiba Prefecture, made by mincing up raw fish – usually horse mackerel or sardines – and adding finely chopped long green onions, root ginger, myoga ginger and miso. 'It's delicious just like that, but the best way to eat it is on top of a bowl of freshly cooked rice,' Yuito had told her. Just hearing about it was enough to make Kotoko's mouth water. She wanted to try it, but Yuito warned her that eating the fish raw was dangerous: 'It might have anisakis.'

Anisakis is a type of roundworm that infests seafood like horse mackerel, mackerel and squid. There is a risk it can be present in fat greenling too, and if you eat the fish raw you can end up with anisakiasis, a parasitic disease that causes severe stomach pain.

'But if you cook it, it's all good!' her brother said. He had made the namero and then piled it into scallop and abalone shells and grilled them. That was another Chiba speciality, called sangayaki. The tantalising smell of charred miso had made Kotoko's stomach rumble. Though she was normally a light eater the grilled fish was so good it had her reaching for seconds of rice too.

But there was one dish she liked even better: simmered fat greenling. Her brother was confident in his mastery of this dish too, and he'd get cocky every time he made it. Kotoko remembered the very first time he had cooked it for her at home. 'Just you wait, I'll serve you the finest simmered fish you've ever eaten.'

'You know how to make it?' Kotoko asked.

'Oh, yeah, piece of cake,' Yuito bragged. In fact, while it took quite a bit of time, it wasn't particularly complicated. You just removed the fat greenling's scales, gills and guts, and then cooked it with all the other sauce ingredients in a frying pan. Yuito always simmered the fish with cooking saké and ginger first, before adding everything else.

'This way makes the flesh more tender. And it gets rid of the fishy smell.' He must have picked this information up somewhere, and he imparted it to Kotoko as though giving a lecture. The saké was meant to enhance the flavour of the greenling. 'Once the alcohol starts to evaporate, we add sugar, soy sauce and mirin, and then just keep it bubbling away. When the sauce goes shiny, it's ready. There – I wouldn't turn my nose up at that in a restaurant, would you?'

Kotoko wouldn't. It was a triumph.

'Yuito, this is so good!'

Kotoko loved it when her brother cooked simmered fish. She asked him to make it for her every time he came home with fat greenling.

'But how did you know this was the right dish?' Kotoko asked Kai. She hadn't mentioned any particular food when she phoned the restaurant. She had been expecting a typical kagezen meal, the usual assortment of small dishes served at a wake or funeral service.

Could it be a coincidence? No – surely not. She had never heard of simmered fat greenling being served as kagezen. Besides, the fish Kai had brought out was cooked just the way her brother used to do it.

'Don't be surprised, Ms Niki,' Kai said. He took out a thick, pocket-sized notebook that looked well-used. 'I have it written down in here.'

'What?'

'Your brother was a regular of ours. I believe he caught fat greenling off the coast around here.'

Of course. Kotoko had forgotten what Kumagai had told her. Now she understood why the dish looked so familiar: her brother had copied the way the restaurant cooked the fish. Maybe he'd asked them how they made it.

But where was the owner? As well as the writing on the chalkboard, which Kotoko had thought was a woman's, she wondered about the embroidery on the apron, but there was no sign of anyone else. Kai seemed to be the only one running the place – or, rather, Kai and Chibi.

Kai put the notebook in the pocket of his apron and began to lay out another set of dishes: Yuito's portion.

'Please take your time, and enjoy.' He bowed his head and returned to the kitchen.

Simmered fat greenling, rice and miso soup – this was the food of Kotoko's memories.

It was so quiet in the restaurant that the ticking of the old clock seemed very loud. From outside the window came the sound of the waves and the mewing of the gulls.

Chibi seemed to have realised he wasn't going to get any of the fat greenling and had curled up on the chair opposite Kotoko, in front of the second serving of the remembrance meal. But there was no sign whatsoever of the departed making an appearance. Kotoko's shoulders slumped. As lovely as this place was, it wasn't what she'd been hoping for. Kumagai had been mistaken. She wasn't going to see Yuito.

With a heavy heart she went through the motions anyway, putting her palms together. 'Itadakimasu,' she said, in appreciation of the meal set out for her. Truthfully she still had no appetite, but it would have been rude not to touch the food. She picked up her chopsticks, determined to eat at least some of the fish.

The fat greenling slipped off the bone easily. The beautiful white flesh was drenched in a translucent brown glaze, and the sweet, tangy aroma of soy sauce and sugar was impossible to resist. She had thought she wasn't hungry, but her stomach gurgled and she found that she wanted to eat.

She popped a piece into her mouth. The first thing that struck her was the flavour of the sauce: both sweet and salty, and with a depth that brought out the taste of the white fish. As she chewed, the flesh of the greenling, light and yet fatty, mingled with the sauce on her tongue and then slowly melted away.

It was mouth-wateringly good, and she couldn't help saying out loud, 'This is even better than the fat greenling Yuito used to make.' But as she murmured this, she tilted her head in confusion: her voice sounded strangely muffled. She wondered if she was getting a cold though her throat felt fine. And even when she was ill, her voice had never sounded like this. Maybe there was something wrong with her ears. *What's happening?* she wondered – and then she heard a man's voice.

'Well, what do you expect from a professional cook?'

The remark seemed to have come in response to Kotoko's words, but it wasn't Kai who had spoken. The voice came from outside the restaurant. And it was a voice she knew. A voice she'd heard nearly every day of her life, until that day in the summer holidays . . .

'It can't be,' Kotoko said to herself. At the same time she heard the clinking of the doorbell. The door to the Chibineko Kitchen opened and she sensed someone come in. She looked up to see a tall, shining figure entering the restaurant.

'*Miaow.*' Chibi jumped down from the seat, as though vacating it for the new arrival, and returned to his place on the rocking chair.

Kotoko caught sight of the old grandfather clock that stood beside Chibi's chair. The pendulum wasn't moving. It had stopped. Something strange was happening. The sound of the waves and the cries of the gulls had faded away. Kotoko couldn't even hear the wind any longer. It was as though time itself had come to a halt.

'What's going on?' she whispered and, as though in answer to her question, the restaurant began to fill with a bright morning mist. Then the figure walked over to her. It was him.

'Hey, Kotoko. How's it going?' He spoke in a voice she knew was Yuito's.

Her brother – her dead brother – was here.

Kotoko had come looking for a miracle, desperate to see Yuito again – but now that he was in front of her, she couldn't speak. She looked round for Kai, hoping he might help her, but there was no sign of him. It was as though Kotoko and Chibi were the only ones who had strayed into this other world.

'Mind if I sit down?' Yuito asked.

Kotoko nodded uncertainly. He sat opposite her, in front of the second portion of the remembrance meal. The food was still steaming.

'Wow! This fat greenling looks tasty,' Yuito said with delight. Though his voice was muffled too, the way he spoke was just the same as when he'd been alive. There was no doubt it was him. Kotoko returned to her senses. If her brother really had appeared, she couldn't just sit here.

'I'll go and fetch Mum and Dad,' she said. She had to bring her parents to see Yuito. They'd be overjoyed; they missed him more than anyone.

It would be quicker to phone, but she wasn't sure she'd be able to explain everything properly. *I'll go home and bring them back here*, she decided, and she was just getting up from her seat when Yuito stopped her.

'Don't.' He seemed to know exactly what Kotoko was thinking.

'Why not?'

'By the time you get back here, I'll be gone.'

'Gone? You mean, you're not staying . . .?'

Her brother shook his head. 'No. I can't be in this world for long. Only until I've finished the food,' he explained.

Then just don't eat! Kotoko began to say, before she suddenly remembered something the chief priest had said at Yuito's funeral.

The departed consume only by scent. We light incense sticks at the altar so the fragrance will provide food for the deceased.

Yuito, who seemed to have read Kotoko's thoughts, was nodding. 'Just think of it as though, for me, the steam is the food.'

So, her brother really was here, but they could only be together as long as the steam continued to rise from the remembrance meal.

'There's something else,' Yuito continued. 'This visit, today, will be my only visit to this world. Once time is up, I don't think I'll be able to come back. We won't be able to speak again.'

I don't think, he had said, but his voice held a steady certainty. He knew this would be their last meeting.

'But that's . . . that's . . .!' Kotoko's voice rose almost to a cry before words failed her. Who was she supposed to direct her frustration towards? She found herself lost in the darkness once again. She'd been nothing *but* lost since her brother had died.

Yuito saw this, and he spoke again as though to console her. 'Even if it *is* just this once, it's still a miracle we get to see each other again at all.'

Kotoko knew this was true, but she couldn't find it in her to agree. She couldn't feel glad. She thought of her mother and father sitting in front of the butsudan, their backs to her. In these last three months they'd both grown smaller, greyer. They must be longing to see Yuito, and now they would never be able to. Kotoko had used up their only chance. She regretted coming alone, regretted coming here without telling them.

'Regretting it won't turn the clock back,' her brother said gently. Harsh as it sounded, he was right. The simmered fat greenling was beginning to cool, the steam growing wispy. The same was happening to the rice and miso soup. At this rate, the food would be stone cold within ten minutes. And then her brother would be gone.

Kotoko panicked. She tried to speak, but her throat was tight and nothing came out. Her mind had gone utterly blank. A little while passed and she still hadn't broken the silence. It was useless. The time with her brother would expire, and she wouldn't have said anything. *I've been given a miracle, and I've squandered it.*

'Here you go.' A voice rang out loud and clear. Kotoko turned to see Kai standing by the table. She thought he'd vanished but here he was after all.

'One more dish for you, Ms Niki,' he said politely, placing the food on the table without even glancing at Yuito.

Two portions again: two bowls of piping-hot rice plus two small dishes containing cubes of jelly, through which the light shone faintly. They were a beautiful colour, like brown garnets or tourmalines.

'Now, this is a real delicacy,' Yuito said, but Kai didn't react. He didn't seem able to see or hear Kotoko's brother.

'A delicacy . . .' Kotoko said quietly, parroting Yuito, and Kai nodded.

'This is one of our specialities,' he said. He could definitely hear Kotoko, then. The knowledge reassured her: it felt as though she had a friend by her side.

'What is it?' she asked, her own voice still indistinct, and Kai explained the cubes to her.

'This is fat greenling nikogori.'

Nikogori is made by chilling fish or meat broth and allowing it to set. It can be made with flounder and other fish naturally rich in gelatine. Sometimes both the broth and the flaked flesh of the simmered fish are set together using agar or another form of edible gelatine. But the nikogori in front of Kotoko now was translucent; it had been made purely from the sauce in which the fish had been cooked.

Kai bowed and left. Presumably he had just gone back to the kitchen, but to Kotoko it seemed as though he'd disappeared into the morning mist. Once again she was alone with her brother. Chibi was asleep on the rocking chair. Occasionally, he mewed a little. He was probably dreaming; cats are supposed to dream in the same way as people.

Then Yuito spoke, as though he'd been waiting until Kai left. 'The nikogori here is seriously good. You should try it on the rice.'

Steam rose from the fresh rice that Kai had placed on the table alongside the exquisite, jewel-like cubes. Kotoko knew she shouldn't be thinking about food at a time like this, but the meal Kai had cooked was so enticing.

'Eat it quickly, or the rice will get cold,' Yuito urged. He seemed eager for his little sister to try some of the delicious dish.

Kotoko nodded and picked up one of the glistening cubes with her chopsticks. It was firm enough that it didn't fall to pieces, but it had a slight wobble to it. She placed it gently on top of the fluffy rice. The nikogori couldn't withstand the heat for long and it slowly melted, releasing the aroma of the simmered fish. The scents of the soy sauce, sugar and fat greenling mingled together, wafting upwards on the steam.

Kotoko scooped up some of the nikogori-soaked rice with her chopsticks and put it in her mouth. As she chewed, the delicate taste of the rice merged with the sweet, tangy sauce and the full-bodied flavour of the fatty fish.

'If the cook doesn't know their stuff, sometimes the nikogori ends up smelling fishy. It can be pretty inedible. But they don't have that problem here – see?' said Yuito, and Kotoko agreed. 'That's because they simmer it properly in saké first,' her brother said, as though he personally was responsible for this. Kotoko couldn't help but find this funny and suddenly the tension lifted: now she could say what it was she wanted to say. She put down her chopsticks and bowed her head to her brother.

'Yuito – I'm sorry,' she said.

'Sorry? What for?'

'For the accident.'

'Oh . . . Kotoko, it wasn't your fault.'

But it *was* her fault. Her brother had given his life to save hers. If Kotoko had been paying more attention to her surroundings, maybe the accident could have been prevented. Maybe Yuito wouldn't have died.

Kotoko had tried telling herself it was the speeding car that was at fault, but it was no good. The other thoughts wouldn't go away; they were constantly on her mind.

'Stop thinking about it,' her brother tried to console her. He had always been there for her. She could remember him helping her time and time again.

When she was still at primary school she had once almost drowned in the sea, and it was her big brother who'd pulled her out. He had protected her from bullies. He'd helped her study. When she told him she couldn't do the horizontal bar in PE, he coached her in the local park. Yuito had even taught her to swim. Whenever she was struggling, he had come to her aid. He had lent her his strength so she wouldn't cry. But now he was gone, and it was her fault.

'I can't,' Kotoko said, her voice trembling. Her words seemed to ring out too loudly. She had dredged them up from the bottom of her heart. 'I can't just stop thinking about it, it's impossible!'

'Maybe,' Yuito acknowledged.

'What should I do?' asked Kotoko.

Ever since the day of the accident, the pain had been unbearable. She'd travelled all this way because she needed her brother to tell her how to go on living without him.

When she looked down at the food, she could see that the steam from the second bowl of rice was starting to peter out. Last time Kai had brought an extra dish, but now there probably wouldn't be another. Her brother had only a little time left in this world.

Yuito was quiet for a while, watching the steam as it began to fade. Maybe it was cruel for someone who was still alive to ask a dead person how to live. Kotoko wondered if her brother would remain silent until the end, but then he spoke.

'I have just one favour to ask you.' His voice was gentle but serious. He didn't seem inclined to answer Kotoko's question. Well, what had she expected? That was what she got for thinking only about herself. Her brother was starting to fade away now too, as though keeping pace with the remembrance meal as it cooled. Kotoko readied herself for their parting.

'What is it?' she asked, urging him to continue. What he said next took her by surprise.

'Act.'

'What?' she asked, failing to understand.

'I want you to go back to the theatre. I want you to perform on stage. That's the favour I'm asking you. And the answer to your question.'

'The answer to my question?'

'Yes. You asked me what you should do, didn't you? Well, you should become an actress.'

Kotoko was baffled. She didn't understand why he'd say something like that. She wanted to question him further, but there was no more time.

'OK, well – I guess it's time to go.' Her brother stood up. In a moment he would be gone and she would never see him again.

Yuito, wait, Kotoko tried to say, but nothing came out. Her lips wouldn't move. Her brother walked towards the restaurant door, leaving Kotoko at the table. Chibi woke from his nap on the rocking chair, jumped down and trotted across the room. He sat himself down daintily at the door and gave a brief mew, as though in goodbye.

'See you,' Yuito said to Chibi, and then the bell clinked again as he opened the door.

It was completely white outside. The sea, the sky, the beach, all were hidden, blanketed in the morning mist. And yet the light was bright – it was like being inside a cloud.

Yuito was about to step through the door and out of Kotoko's sight. She summoned all her strength to call out to him.

'Yuito!'

Without turning round, he answered. 'Thanks for coming, Kotoko. I'll be watching over you. I'll always be with you. I'm a part of you.'

And with those final words, he passed through the door.

It must have been only a few seconds later when Kotoko realised that the world had returned to normal: the mist had cleared and the old clock was still ticking away. It was as though she'd been dreaming – except there was Chibi sitting beside the slightly open door. Her brother had gone without closing it behind him.

His words were left ringing in Kotoko's ears.

I want you to go back to the theatre . . . I want you to perform on stage . . . You should become an actress.

Did he mean he wanted Kotoko to find fame in his stead? She couldn't think of any other explanation, but she sensed that wasn't it. Her brother wasn't the kind of person who would entrust his dream to someone else. *Let alone foist it onto his little sister*, she thought.

As Kotoko was pondering this, Chibi came over to her chair mewing. He peered up at her face and mewed again insistently.

Kotoko felt as though Chibi was trying to tell her something but, unlike her brother, she couldn't speak cat. Still, she looked down at the kitten trying to glean some sort of clue. *Come on, tell me, Chibi. Why did Yuito say those things?* He didn't respond, but then Kotoko heard footsteps.

'Some green tea to finish off with, Ms Niki.'

Kai was back, as courteous and softly spoken as before. He placed the tea on the table and was about to return to the kitchen when Kotoko called him back.

'Could I ask you something?'

'Certainly,' Kai replied. He was the only person in the world Kotoko could question about what had just happened. She wanted him to solve the riddle for her, to tell her the meaning of Yuito's words.

'I saw my brother,' she began, and then she told Kai everything that had occurred. 'Why do you think he might have said that?'

There was a long silence. To Kotoko it seemed less as though Kai was puzzling over her question and more as though he was debating whether or not he should give her the answer.

'Please,' she pressed him, and finally Kai replied.

'I can only offer you my thoughts on what your brother might have meant. Are you sure you wish to hear them?'

'Yes.'

Kai watched as Kotoko nodded and then he began to unravel the mystery.

'I wonder if, perhaps, your brother wishes to take to the stage once more himself,' he said.

'But what does *me* going on stage have to do with . . .' Kotoko began, and then suddenly her brother's words came back to her.

I'll always be with you. I'm a part of you.

If that were true, then when Kotoko was performing, her brother would be up there beside her. Perhaps he wanted to look out from the stage into an audience once again. In fact she was sure of it. He'd been so intent on going into acting, he'd even dropped out of university – it made sense that there were still things he wanted to achieve. And of course, he wasn't one to be satisfied with a mere bit part. He had been the heart of the theatre company. He had stood centre stage.

'I'll rejoin Yuito's theatre group,' Kotoko said. It would be for her own sake, as much as her brother's.

She thought that she might like to stand centre stage too. Maybe, deep down, she had always wanted to act.

And this way, she would never forget Yuito. As life went on, the days she'd spent with her brother would fade into the past. But if Kotoko became an actress, they would always be together. As long as she was acting, she would be following in his footsteps.

Those fears she'd once had – *I could never do it, I can't do anything* – had vanished. She wanted to begin training as soon as possible.

'I'm going to go back to acting,' she told Kai.

'The very best of luck. Chibi and I will be with you all the way.'

Chibi swished his tail to and fro as though in complete agreement.

It was just after ten in the morning, and so time for the restaurant to close. Kotoko had been the only customer: perhaps they didn't accept other diners when they were serving a remembrance meal.

The kagezen hadn't been cheap, but neither was it outrageously expensive. If you considered that you were booking the whole room, the price seemed fair. Kotoko paid her bill and bowed to Kai and Chibi.

'Thank you very much for the meal.'

She opened the door with its clinking bell and stepped outside, where the brilliant blue of the sea and sky stretched out to infinity. The black-tailed gulls ambled about on the sand as though they had nothing better to do. A pleasant breeze was blowing.

'Please take care of your hat,' Kai said. He had come out to see her off but Chibi had remained indoors – no doubt to avoid a further scolding.

'Yes, I'll hold on to it tight this time,' Kotoko replied, pulling it down firmly on her head.

The white seashell path lay before her. She'd met Kai here only an hour or so earlier. An encounter that would change her life.

I'm glad I came to this seaside town. I'm glad I visited the Chibineko Kitchen, Kotoko thought. She was content, but before she returned to Tokyo, there was one more thing she wanted to find out. She plucked up the courage to ask the question.

'Could I come back again? Not for kagezen, just a normal meal . . .' Her voice sounded very timid. She feared Kai would laugh at her for wanting to travel all this way just for a meal, but his reply was gracious.

'Of course,' he said, 'please come back whenever you like. We'll be expecting you, and we'll make sure we have something delicious prepared.'

So, Kotoko could see Kai and Chibi again. She looked forward to that day.

A special recipe from the Chibineko Kitchen

Namero-don: Seasoned minced fish served on rice

Ingredients (serves 2)

- Raw horse mackerel or sardine (or any other fish that is safe to eat raw as sashimi). If using horse mackerel, 3 fish should be enough.
- Condiments of your choice e.g. long green onions (negi) or spring onions, green shiso leaf, root ginger, myoga ginger, sesame seeds – to taste
- Miso, soy sauce – to taste
- 2 bowls of rice, freshly cooked

Method

1. Fillet the fish and then coarsely chop the flesh using a kitchen knife.

2. Finely chop the long green onions, shiso and the other condiments.
3. Mix the fish and condiments together on the chopping board and continue mincing the mixture until it is well combined. Mix in the miso and soy sauce.
4. Serve on top of the freshly cooked rice.

Tips

You can use whichever fish and condiments you like, as this is home cooking. Add just a dash of soy sauce at first and then pour more over at the end, seasoning to taste. You can also enjoy namero-don topped with an onsen tamago (slow-cooked egg).

2

A black cat and a sandwich from a first love

たまご

Eggs

Chiba Prefecture is an important region for egg production in Japan. The chickens raised there are fed on seafood and seaweed in addition to vegetables, soybeans and corn. The resulting eggs are sweet and rich, with the perfect flavour for making baked goods and ice cream, as well as savoury dishes.

At Mitsunaga Farm in Kimitsu, on the Boso Peninsula, the eggs have particularly deep-orange yolks.

The spring holiday was over and Taiji Hashimoto had just started his fifth year of primary school. Some of his classmates spent all their time playing video games, but not Taiji. He had better things to do.

After his lessons ended for the day, he went straight on to a session at cram school. He had mountains of homework to finish and, on top of that, he was busy revising for his mock exams. To get into his first choice of private junior high school he would have to pass an entrance exam. The advanced evening and weekend classes his parents paid for would help him prepare for this. Still, he didn't mind studying, and though it was tiring, he never took even a single day off.

A new pupil had just started at the cram school, a girl called Fumika Nakazato who the teacher told them had recently moved to the area. Taiji didn't take much notice: people were always joining and dropping out of the class, and it wasn't as though anyone was there to make friends anyway.

But then something happened that forced Taiji to pay attention. In the very first test she took, Fumika came second, only three marks below him, and she had actually beaten him in the Japanese and social studies sections. It was the first time anyone had threatened to knock Taiji off his perch at the top of the class.

Suddenly everyone was talking about her. 'That new girl Fumika is so smart!' Taiji kept hearing classmates say. She had made a big impression, appearing from nowhere and getting such outstanding marks.

Taiji was as surprised as everyone else and he started to take notice of Fumika. She looked like one of his favourite pop singers, he thought. But he never tried to speak to her; talking to girls didn't come easily. A month went by and they still hadn't exchanged a word.

In order to give the pupils extra revision time, every few weeks the cram school also ran on a Sunday. Taiji's parents were always too busy to make him a packed lunch, so instead they gave him money for bread or rice balls from the nearby convenience store.

On this particular Sunday, the bread and rice balls that Taiji liked best were sold out. There were some bento lunches left, but as he planned to take his food to the park he didn't want to bother with chopsticks. In the end he settled on just a packet of cookies and a carton of coffee-flavoured milk. It would be more like a snack than lunch, but he didn't mind – studying always gave him an appetite for something sweet.

The park behind the school was generally quiet. Sometimes there was a black cat, and Taiji had also seen people from the local theatre group doing voice exercises, but mostly when Taiji went there to eat he was the only one, and he thought of the park as his private lunch spot. But not this time. There was no cat, or anyone from the theatre group. Instead, there was Fumika Nakazato sitting on a bench with a picnic basket and a flask of soup on her lap.

'Oh, great,' Taiji muttered with annoyance. There were only two benches and the other was broken. He hadn't expected anyone else to be here, and now he could think of only three options: eat standing up, look for somewhere else or go back to the classroom. As he tried to make up his mind, Fumika called over to him.

'Aren't you going to eat?'

'Yes, but . . .' He was unnerved by her. When he crossed paths with the girls at school, he tended to ignore them and they acted as though they hadn't seen him either. But now Fumika was speaking directly to him. He stood there in silence.

'Do you want to sit here?' Fumika asked, motioning for him to join her on the bench. Taiji grew even more flustered. He thought about telling her he was OK standing, but that would show her how awkward he felt around her, which would be a disaster too.

'All right then,' Taiji said, sitting down next to Fumika as though it was no big deal. He immediately regretted it: the bench wasn't long and there was hardly any space between them. He was close enough to reach out and touch her. His heart was racing so badly that he worried Fumika might actually hear it thumping.

She, on the other hand, seemed cool and collected. Taiji's gaze fell on her picnic basket as she opened it and he saw that it contained sandwiches – egg sandwiches. They clearly weren't shop-bought.

Fumika must have noticed him staring, because she held the picnic basket out to him. 'You can have one, if you want. I think they turned out pretty well!'

Taiji looked at the sandwiches with surprise. 'Did you make them yourself?' They seemed so perfect he could hardly believe it.

'Yes. I mean, my mum cooked the eggs. But I put them in the bread,' Fumika replied. She had a mischievous look on her face and Taiji realised she was teasing him. He burst out laughing.

'Hey, that's cheating! That's not making them yourself!'

'Maybe you're right,' Fumika said seriously before dissolving into giggles.

'*Maybe?* I'm definitely right!'

It was the first time he had ever talked to a girl like this, but now that they'd shared a joke the tension had lifted. His heart was still pounding, but it felt different from before.

'Can I really have one?' he asked.

'Of course.'

'Thanks,' Taiji replied as he reached for a sandwich. His hand closed around the firm bread and as he brought it to his mouth, he caught the buttery, eggy scent. He wolfed it down and then gave Fumika his assessment.

'That was *really good*.'

'You mean it? I'll tell my mum, she'll be so happy. Thanks, Taiji.'

At the time, Taiji didn't question why Fumika had thanked him or why it would make her mum especially happy.

The cram school didn't give the pupils long for lunch. By the time Taiji had eaten the sandwich, it was only ten minutes until the afternoon lessons started.

The thick pumpkin soup in Fumika's flask was steaming invitingly but she screwed the lid back on and returned it to her basket.

'There's no time to eat it,' she explained, getting ready to go. She was right – if they didn't leave now, they'd be late.

They were both heading to the same classroom but Taiji was too shy to walk back with her, and she seemed to feel similarly.

'I'll go back first,' Taiji said; Fumika gave a little nod.

'OK.'

'Well, see you . . .'

Taiji was about to stand up when he suddenly realised he still had the things he'd bought at the shop. He hesitated for a moment, then opened the packet of cookies and held it out to Fumika.

'You can have one – in return for the sandwich.' He meant it as a thank you.

But Fumika didn't react in the way he'd expected. She glanced at the cookies and then back up at Taiji in dismay.

'Thanks, but I . . .' She started to say something but Taiji couldn't bring himself to listen: she was turning him down. He felt his cheeks redden.

It wasn't as though he'd asked her out or anything – all he'd done was offer her a cookie – and yet he felt as though he had been rejected. And they had sat on the bench together, joking and laughing! She had given him a sandwich! He thought they had been getting on well – he thought they were friends. And yet now she was looking at him as if he'd done something peculiar.

Taiji didn't say anything else, just shoved the packet of cookies into his pocket and ran out of the park.

'Taiji . . .' he heard Fumika call, but he didn't stop.

'Hey, Taiji, are you and Fumika going out?' Tamura asked as soon as Taiji had returned to the classroom and taken his seat.

Tamura never got good marks. He was always messing around in class, playing games on his phone or reading manga. Taiji thought Tamura was an idiot; if he didn't want to study, why didn't he just leave cram school, instead of wasting his time and his parents' money?

Normally Taiji would take no notice of him, but this time was different.

'What?' Taiji asked curtly.

'Weren't you sitting with her earlier?' Tamura grinned.

He saw us. Taiji's heart lurched. He was sure Tamura was going to make fun of him. He remembered the look on Fumika's face as she refused his offer. *It was only a cookie, why couldn't she have just taken it?* The thought made him angry, so he scowled and said: 'I am *not* going out with her. We just ended up sitting on the same bench, that's all.'

Taiji's words were blunt, but it was true enough.

‘So you don’t fancy her then?’ said Tamura.

In the face of this teasing, Taiji said something uncalled for. He said it loudly, too: ‘Of course I don’t fancy her! Actually I hate her. She’s ugly. I don’t even like talking to her.’

At that moment the classroom fell completely silent. Taiji’s classmates looked towards the door. There was Fumika, standing in the doorway.

‘Now you’ve done it,’ said Tamura.

She had heard every word.

I shouldn’t have said those things. I shouldn’t have said I hated her, or that she was ugly or that I didn’t like talking to her. At the very least I should have said sorry straight away, Taiji thought over and over again. But it was too late. The next day Fumika didn’t turn up to school. She was off for a few days and then Taiji heard that she’d left. He wondered, with a sinking feeling, if her sudden disappearance had anything to do with his cruel words.

He wanted to speak to Fumika, to ask her why she’d gone, but he didn’t know her address, or phone number or Line ID. He tried looking her up on social media but he only found other people with the same name. They didn’t have any friends in common either so he had no way of contacting her. Taiji felt as though a gaping hole had opened up in his chest. There was no one he could turn to.

Days, weeks, months went by and then primary school ended for the summer holidays. But the classes at the cram school ramped up as the date of the junior high school entrance exams crept closer. Several children – Tamura among them – dropped out, unable to keep up with the lessons.

Taiji was still scoring top marks. Other pupils sometimes made fun of him for being a swot but he paid them no attention; answering back was a waste of time and anyway, he enjoyed learning.

Taiji was set on getting a place at his chosen school. But there was something else driving him to sign up for one mock exam after another. He got on trains and travelled to exam centres across the city hoping that maybe, somewhere, he might come across Fumika who would surely be preparing for entrance exams too. Failing that, he hoped to get his name published on the list of top scorers, where she might see it. He scoured the lists for her name too.

But it was no good. The weeks of searching were fruitless. Fumika had vanished like a wisp of smoke. It was as though she had never existed.

*

When people disappear, the world keeps on turning. Time doesn't stop. The summer of cram school came to an end. While Taiji had been immersed in his studies, the year had crept on and now it was nearly November. Every day seemed like a repeat of the previous day – but, little by little, things were changing.

Taiji and his classmates would start their final year of primary school the following spring, and so the cram school had begun holding meetings with pupils to discuss their plans. Taiji's marks were excellent and it was already decided that he would be placed in the top class.

'Keep it up like this, and you'll be fine,' his teacher told him, just as he had at their previous meeting. 'Just make sure you stay focused.'

'OK. I'll try my best,' Taiji replied. The teacher was in his forties, and he had been at the school for as long as Taiji. Taiji didn't dislike him, but he didn't feel particularly close to him either, and he hoped that would be the end of their conversation. He just wanted to be left on his own. But the teacher wasn't finished. As though broaching the real subject of the meeting, he said with concern, 'Tell me, Taiji, have you been feeling tired recently? You're not under the weather?'

'I'm fine,' Taiji answered. It wasn't a lie, he didn't have a cold or any kind of physical illness, it was just that he had no appetite and was losing weight. Taiji's parents were worried and had taken him to the hospital but the doctor had found nothing wrong. It wasn't Taiji's body that was sick – it was his spirit. Since Fumika had gone there'd been a tightness, a pain deep in his chest. Sometimes he cried when he was alone. But he didn't intend to tell any of this to his teacher.

'Well, perhaps it's tough for you not having any real competition here,' the teacher said, nodding as though satisfied by his own explanation. Then he added casually: 'If only Fumika Nakazato were still with us, she could have given you a run for your money.'

Taiji froze in astonishment. Fumika was the last person he had expected to come up in conversation. The teacher, missing the shock on Taiji's face, continued speaking, almost to himself. 'What a tragic thing, passing away so young like that . . .'

'What?' Taiji asked hesitantly. He didn't understand. Maybe he had misheard. 'Who . . . Who's passed away?'

'You mean you didn't know?' The teacher looked alarmed, as though he had said something he shouldn't have. Then, seeing Taiji's confusion, he sighed and said: 'Fumika Nakazato. She passed away.'

'What?' Taiji asked again, not wanting to believe it.

'Don't you remember her – the girl who came second in that test? I'm afraid she died.'

'When?' asked Taiji.

'Not long after she stopped coming to lessons.'

'But . . . But why?'

'Well, she was ill. She had been for quite some time.'

The teacher looked at Taiji and finally seemed to realise how much the subject was affecting him. He began to explain, telling Taiji things about Fumika he had never known.

Fumika's heart had been weak since birth and she spent more time in hospital than she did at home. Though she had a satchel full of textbooks, she hadn't attended primary school even for a single day.

The human body is a mysterious thing, and while there was no prospect of Fumika's recovery, there were times when she appeared quite well. She told her parents and her doctors that when she was well enough she wanted to go to school, just like any other child – she wanted to make friends. The only people Fumika had to talk to were her parents and the medical staff.

Though there were lots of other children on the ward, many of them were very ill and might not live much longer, and the thought of getting to know them was too sad.

Fumika's parents felt extremely sorry for their daughter but they were worried that school would be too taxing for her. She wouldn't be able to go in every day or join in with PE. They weren't even sure if any school would accept her. Still, she begged them again and again to let her try, so they spoke to the doctors and at last everyone agreed that Fumika could go to a cram school rather than an ordinary one. It would be more flexible and the hours would work better for her.

'What do you think?' Fumika's father asked her.

'What if I can't keep up?' Fumika looked anxious, but her father had no worries on that score.

'You'll be fine,' he reassured her. Though Fumika had never been to school, she had kept up with her studies at home and in hospital, working through textbooks and attending remote-learning classes. Her parents knew she'd been applying herself, motivated by her dream of going to school.

In the end, even though her wish only half came true, Fumika was delighted by the decision.

'Do you think I'll make any friends?' she asked her parents and the doctors, excited but nervous. She told them about how she wanted someone to chat to, someone to sit next to and eat lunch with. Hearing Fumika talk like this, her parents struggled to hold back their tears. They knew their daughter's life would soon be cut short.

As the teacher was speaking, the tightness in Taiji's chest worsened. When the meeting was over, he dashed into a toilet cubicle and cried.

All the things the teacher had told him, the image of Fumika studying in a hospital bed, her excitement at being able to attend cram school, raced round and round inside his head. She was sick and he'd said he hated her. She'd hoped to make friends and he'd hurt her. *I'm sorry*, he apologised silently. But it was much too late. No matter how many times he said he was sorry, his words would never reach Fumika. For the first time, Taiji learned that there are things in life that can never be undone.

Taiji was on his way home. He was walking past the park where he'd sat on the bench with Fumika, when he heard someone chanting what sounded like a strange magic spell: '. . . but those of you who do not know it, you must be swallowing real peppercorns whole, you must be riding the night boat down the Shirakawa, and so let me take one pill to show you what it does . . .'

It was 'The Medicine Peddler' speech from a kabuki play and Taiji had heard it before because the theatre company who sometimes practised in the park used it as an exercise to help the actors train their voices. He presumed the young woman reciting was a member of the troupe.

Beside her was the black cat Taiji often saw. It had a beautiful, sleek coat and it was sitting on its haunches watching her. It looked aloof, as though it were supervising a lesson.

'*Miaow,*' the cat mewed when it saw Taiji. The girl stopped mid-chant and looked round.

'Oh, hello Taiji.'

Taiji recognised her: it was Kotoko Niki who he'd known for as long as he could remember. She had always lived in his neighbourhood and she'd been his home tutor, too, for a short while. About three months ago, Taiji had heard that Kotoko's brother had died in a car accident, but she seemed in good spirits now.

He was worried he'd interrupted her practice, but Kotoko didn't seem to mind at all.

'Are you on your way home from cram school?' she asked.

'Yes.'

'Must be tough?'

'No, it's all right,' Taiji replied. And then, as he looked up at Kotoko, something in her face reminded him of Fumika. That was all it took to reduce him to tears. He was embarrassed at weeping in public like this, but he couldn't stop. Kotoko's eyes widened in surprise at this sudden show of emotion. 'What's wrong?' she asked, concerned.

'She . . . She's dead!' Taiji replied, his chest heaving. Between sobs he told Kotoko all about Fumika. Kotoko stood quietly until Taiji had finished speaking, and then she said something unexpected.

'Have you ever heard of a remembrance meal?'

Taiji had never heard the term. It sounded like something from a manga or a storybook and he said this to Kotoko, who explained: 'When you eat a remembrance meal at the Chibineko Kitchen, you might be able to hear the voice of someone who's important to you.'

'Someone important to me?' said Taiji.

'Yes. For me, it was my brother.'

'What? But . . .'

'That's right. He died. But I saw him. I went to the Chibineko Kitchen and spoke to him,' said Kotoko.

'What . . .? How . . .?' Taiji was dumbstruck.

'You might not believe me, but it's true,' Kotoko continued. It sounded impossible, yet Taiji wanted to believe that there was a place where you could go to talk to someone who had died. A place where he could talk to Fumika.

'*Miaow.*' The black cat mewed at Taiji and Kotoko and then, flicking its tail carelessly from side to side, walked out of the park. *I'm off*, it seemed to be saying. They watched it leave, and then as though she'd just remembered something, Kotoko said: 'Taiji, are you OK with cats? You're not allergic or anything?'

'N . . . No.' Taiji shook his head, puzzled. He'd never had a pet cat, but he didn't mind them. Kotoko gave a relieved smile.

'Then you'll be fine!'

'What do you mean?' asked Taiji.

'The Chibineko Kitchen has a cat.'

After saying goodbye to Kotoko and the black cat, Taiji ran home. His parents weren't back from work yet so he was alone in the house. There would be a snack for him in the fridge but he didn't even bother looking – instead he dashed straight to his room and began searching on his phone for the Chibineko Kitchen.

Kotoko had told him the restaurant was in Uchibo and she'd given him their number, but he wanted to find out more before calling. The Chibineko Kitchen didn't seem to have a website and it wasn't on any review sites either, but Taiji came across a blog by a lady who said she was writing from her hospital bed. At the top of the page, in letters that looked as if they were written in chalk, the blog's title read:

Remembrance Meals
at the Chibineko Kitchen

There was a counter that showed the number of people who had visited the blog, and the total was surprisingly low, yet still it captured Taiji's attention. Maybe it was because he'd just found out that Fumika had spent so much time in hospital too, and he felt as though he would learn something important from reading on.

My husband went missing a long time ago.
Twenty years ago now.
He went out to sea to fish, and he never came back.

It continued:

> There's no way he's still alive. I should give him up for lost. That's what the police and the local fishermen have told me. But I still can't abandon hope. When we got married, my husband said to me: 'I'll be the one who lives longest. I'll always be there to take care of you.' That's what he promised me. And I believe him. He wouldn't die before me and leave me and our child behind.

Taiji kept reading. After her husband's disappearance, the lady had opened a restaurant in order to support herself and had named it the 'Chibineko Kitchen', because the family had a chibineko – a little cat. It was a sweet name, and quite unusual too, but it wasn't the name that had kept the Chibineko Kitchen in business: it was the fact that their food had a special selling point.

'I managed to earn a living thanks to the remembrance meals I served – the kagezen,' the restaurant owner explained.

Taiji looked up 'kagezen' and found that it had two meanings: the food you offered up for someone who was away from home, and the food you put out when mourning the dead. The first meaning was the original one but now kagezen was more often used to refer to the food offered up when someone died. It was something Taiji had seen for himself at a family funeral.

As well as the regular menu, the restaurant's owner had begun preparing kagezen meals to pray for her husband's safety. When her diners saw this, they started requesting kagezen in memory of their own late family and friends. Lots of people, it turned out, wanted to use food as a way of remembering those dear to them, even if it wasn't at a funeral.

The lady called these offerings 'remembrance meals'. She would ask the diner for their memories of the departed and then cook something to remind them of their loved one. Then, the blog continued, a miracle happened – something unbelievable. She put her heart and soul into the preparation of each remembrance meal, and as they ate, the diners found that memories of their loved ones came flooding back. But that wasn't all. They actually heard their voices – there were even those who said they had spoken to the dead. The blog's author wasn't sure whether or not to believe what her diners told her, since she had never heard or seen anything unusual herself. Either the miracle only occurred for the person who ate the remembrance meal or the diners were enjoying a collective joke.

But Taiji believed it – after all, people could work miracles. And he wanted to think there could be a way for him to see Fumika again.

Something bothered him, though. The website hadn't been updated for over a month. It gave no clues as to why the lady was in hospital and maybe she was seriously ill. But Taiji decided to stop speculating. He had made up his mind to put his faith in the restaurant so he took a deep breath and phoned the number Kotoko had given him. After two rings a young man answered.

'This is the Chibineko Kitchen. Thank you very much for your call.'

His voice was soft. He didn't sound scary at all. Taiji was relieved and said, 'I'd like to book a remembrance meal.'

He'd never made a reservation at a restaurant before, and he was worried he might be refused because of his age.

But the reply came instantly. 'Certainly.'

I'll get to see Fumika, Taiji thought.

'It's Mr Taiji Hashimoto, isn't it?' asked the young man.

Taiji was surprised: 'How do you know my name?'

'Ms Niki mentioned you to me,' the man explained. What had seemed strange only seconds ago now made sense: Kotoko must have phoned the restaurant. Taiji didn't mind, though, because it had helped the call go smoothly.

'Yes, that's right, I'm Taiji Hashimoto,' he confirmed. The man said the restaurant was only open in the morning, but that suited Taiji. Getting there late at night would have been much more complicated.

Everything was settled, and Taiji was about to hang up, when the man said hastily: 'We have a cat at the Chibineko Kitchen, is that all right?'

Taiji already knew about the cat from Kotoko. 'Of course,' he said – and with that, his visit was arranged for the following Sunday.

And now Sunday had arrived. Taiji hadn't been in touch with Kotoko to let her know he was going even though she had offered to accompany him. He also had no intention of telling his parents; he felt this was something he should do by himself.

'I've got another mock exam today,' Taiji lied to them. He genuinely did have an exam, but he was going to miss it. His parents didn't suspect a thing.

They wished him luck and gave him his train fare and lunch money. But that wouldn't be enough – the restaurant was much further away than the exam venue and the meal would cost more. Taiji took the pocket money he'd been saving up and slipped it into his wallet.

He'd made sure he knew the details of the ninety-minute journey from Tokyo station to the seaside town, and he wasn't worried about it; compared with navigating the Tokyo underground, it would be easy.

Tokyo station was bustling with people but Taiji found his way on to his train without any difficulty. The carriage was surprisingly quiet, and he settled into a seat next to the door. He thought about reading more of the blog but he'd be in big trouble if his battery died and he needed his phone to find the restaurant. So he just sat there until he began to drift off; his nerves had stopped him from sleeping well the previous night.

When he woke from his nap, he found that the train had pulled in at a station and the carriage was completely empty. Everyone must have got out already. Taiji rushed onto the platform and stood still. He couldn't smell the sea, or see any sign of it. He *was* at the coast, wasn't he? He began to panic that he'd got off at the wrong place, but the name on the signs was right.

'This has to be it,' he muttered to himself as he went

through the ticket barrier and walked towards the bus stop in front of the station. The old bus arrived on time, and when Taiji boarded, he found it was almost empty – there were only two other passengers: an old man and woman who he assumed to be husband and wife.

The driver announced the bus's destination and then they were off. After about five minutes they pulled up outside a large hospital where the elderly couple got out, leaving Taiji on his own. Three stops later, he got off too. Card payments weren't accepted so he was glad that he'd brought cash, but nonetheless he was a little anxious as he handed over his fare, never having paid a bus driver using coins before.

Taiji had travelled quite a long way now but the Chibineko Kitchen was further still – a fifteen-minute walk from the bus stop according to the map on his phone. In an unfamiliar neighbourhood in Tokyo he would worry about getting lost, but here the Koitogawa River, which flowed into Tokyo Bay, marked his route. If Taiji followed the road that ran alongside it, he'd reach the sea, and there he would find the restaurant.

'Nearly there. I'll see her soon,' Taiji said out loud. The thought of Fumika made his chest hurt as though it were being squeezed. Trying to shake off the feeling, he set off down the riverside road.

The sea really was close: it came into view when Taiji had walked for only five minutes. Just then, he heard a cry: '*miaoow, miaoow*'. For a moment he thought it was a cat but the sound had come from overhead, and he looked up to see a bird calling out as it soared above him.

'A sea cat?' he wondered, but he wasn't sure if that was right. He only knew the name and the noise they were supposed to make. He stopped to search the dictionary on his phone.

Black-tailed gull, 'sea cat'

A gull in the Laridae family of seabirds. It inhabits the coastlines and islands of Japan and the surrounding region, and has a white body, a dark-grey back and wings and a black tail. It is known as the 'sea cat' due to its call which sounds like the mewing of a cat.

Taiji wondered what made these birds different from other gulls. Another search revealed that whereas the common gull's beak is plain yellow, the black-tailed gull's has a black-and-red tip. The common gull's cry is different too, and doesn't sound so much like a cat.

Happy to have his hunch confirmed, Taiji put his phone back in his pocket and set off again down the road by the Koitogawa. It was remarkably quiet. The riverside road snaked along an embankment lined by a row of elegant old houses, but there was no sign of anyone and no passing cars either. The silence was broken only by the cat-like mewing of the gulls.

Taiji walked on until he could smell salt in the air; the gulls' cries grew louder and he could hear the waves. When he reached an empty beach stretching off into the distance, he let out an 'oh' of surprise. Born and brought up in Tokyo, he had never seen anything like it. The only footprints in the sand were his own.

After a few minutes he came to a path strewn with white seashells. 'I hope it's OK to step on them,' Taiji murmured, reluctant to crush such beautiful objects. But this was definitely the path the map showed he should take, so he walked cautiously along its edge until a building came into sight. This must be the Chibineko Kitchen. He was finally here.

Taiji dashed forwards. He was surprised to find there was no sign above the door but he knew he was in the right place when he read the writing on the small chalkboard outside:

The Chibineko Kitchen
We serve remembrance meals.

Taiji was concerned as to whether or not he would be allowed inside – it wasn't like a family restaurant or a food court at the supermarket. Would they really let a child eat alone in such a grown-up place? It had been his decision to come here on his own, but now he wasn't sure he had the courage to step inside. As he hesitated by the door, he heard a sound coming from behind the chalkboard.

'*Miaow.*'

This time, it wasn't a seagull. Taiji peered round behind the board and there, looking up at him from its hiding place, was a kitten. This must be the restaurant's cat that Kotoko had mentioned to him. He was about to say something to the little cat when the doorbell clinked, the door opened and a young man emerged.

He wore narrow-framed glasses and had delicate good looks like the pop idols Taiji saw on TV. Spotting Taiji, the man said, 'You must be Mr Hashimoto?'

Taiji recognised the courteous, soft voice from his phone call.

'Y . . . Yes,' he stammered and the man bowed.

'Thank you very much for booking a table with us. My name is Kai Fukuchi – it's a pleasure to meet you. Welcome to the Chibineko Kitchen.'

Taiji was suddenly lost for words. Though relieved at not being shooed away, he was still nervous talking to this polite stranger.

But Kai didn't remark on Taiji's shyness. Instead he simply said: 'We're ready for you. Please, come in,' and opened the door wide for Taiji like a friendly butler from a manga, setting the bell clinking again.

Taiji opened his mouth to thank Kai, but before he could speak, a sound came from down by his feet.

'*Miaow*,' the cat mewed, looking up at Kai. It was so sweet that Taiji couldn't help giving a slight smile, but Kai's mouth didn't even twitch.

'Now, I have *told* you, you mustn't go outside. Do you understand?' he said reproachfully. Taiji noticed how formally Kai spoke even when addressing the kitten. It reminded him of Kotoko's way of speaking. But Kai was, if anything, even more polite.

'*Miaow*,' the kitten responded, and then he stuck his tail in the air and trotted into the restaurant as though he owned the place. He didn't seem particularly perturbed by the telling-off. Kai sighed and then bowed his head to Taiji.

'Our restaurant cat, Chibi. I do hope he didn't trouble you.'

'N . . . Not at all.'

Then, as though he needed to take charge of the situation, Kai said: 'Please do come in.'

'Thank you,' said Taiji as politely as he could, and followed Chibi through the door.

Inside the restaurant his gaze was immediately drawn to the window in the far wall which was large enough for a person to step through. Just beyond was the sea, with the black-tailed gulls circling above. The beach was still deserted – Taiji wondered if it was because it was still morning, or because it was too late in the year for swimming. The sound of the waves was constant, soothing.

Taiji was the only customer so it was quiet inside and he had plenty of opportunity to look round at the old grandfather clock in the corner and the rocking chair. He wondered if the chair was Chibi's favourite spot, as by now the kitten had clambered up onto it, curled into a ball and sunk into what looked like a very pleasant nap.

There was no sign of the lady who had written the blog; Kai seemed to be the only person there. Once he had shown Taiji to his table he said, 'Your meal will be ready soon,' and then he disappeared into the kitchen leaving Taiji all alone. There was no TV and Taiji didn't feel like looking at his phone, so he gazed at Chibi and at the view from the window. After about ten minutes Kai returned carrying a tray laden with soup and sandwiches.

'I apologise for keeping you waiting,' he said, placing not one but two helpings of food on the table. 'Please could you let me know if this all matches your request?'

Taiji looked closely and nodded. The sandwiches were filled with generous slices of rolled omelette – no ordinary egg mayonnaise, no ham or cheese or anything else. A sweet aroma wafted up from the soup. *This* was what Fumika had been eating that day in the park.

'Thick omelette sandwiches and pumpkin soup,' Kai confirmed. 'Please, enjoy them.'

'*Miaow.*' Enticed by the smell, Chibi had woken up and his nose was twitching.

'O . . . OK,' said Taiji, reaching for a sandwich.

Hearing another mew, this time from by his feet, he looked down to see that Chibi had crept up close. To his surprise, the little cat seemed to want some of the sandwiches.

'Sorry,' he said to Chibi, as he picked up a hefty sandwich. The rolled omelette between the slices of bread was warm and looked a good five centimetres thick.

Until Fumika had shared her lunch with him, Taiji had never heard of a rolled omelette sandwich. But he'd looked it up online afterwards and learned that it had been invented by a traditional Japanese cafe called Amanoya and had since been featured on TV programmes and in magazines. Apparently lots of families made it at home.

Taiji visualised the scene in the park again. Fumika sitting there on the bench, picnic basket on her lap. And here was his remembrance meal. When he ate these sandwiches, he would see her. His heart started to beat faster. One part of him wanted to speak to her as soon as he could, but the other part wanted to flee the restaurant.

'*Miaow*,' Chibi mewed, as though telling him to hurry up and eat before the food got cold.

'OK, I get it,' he said to the little cat and, with his feelings still in turmoil, he took a bite. As he chewed, the taste of the thick white bread filled his mouth, aromatic and slightly sweet. It had been lightly toasted and buttered. Next, the flavour of the filling came through. The omelette was seasoned with dashi, as well as plenty of mustard and mayonnaise, which drew out the mild sweetness of the egg. It melted deliciously in Taiji's mouth. It might have been the tastiest thing he had eaten since Fumika had died. But after the first mouthful he stopped eating. Disappointment coursed through him. He put the sandwich down on the plate.

'It's not right,' he said to Kai.

It wasn't the sandwich Fumika had shared with him that day. It looked identical but something was different. He could tell after only one bite. And though he strained his ears, Taiji couldn't hear Fumika's voice. She wasn't here. This wasn't her remembrance meal.

Taiji thought Kai might argue with him – adults never admitted when they got things wrong – but he just murmured, 'Ah, so that's it then,' as though something had been confirmed. Taiji wanted to ask what he meant but Kai continued.

'I do apologise. I hope you won't mind waiting a few more minutes.' He bowed and then slipped away into the kitchen before Taiji could reply. Chibi watched him go, his ears twitching curiously.

Taiji was curious too. He wondered whether Kai was angry at having his cooking rejected by a child. But the handsome young man who was courteous to children and cats alike hadn't let his polite demeanour slip for even a moment.

'Don't you think your owner is kind of strange?' Taiji asked the kitten. Chibi lowered his head and gave a little mew in agreement. In fact Kai wasn't the only one who was strange, Taiji thought: it was as though the little kitten could understand him and they were having a proper conversation.

Ten minutes later, Kai returned. He set out the dishes on the table – two portions again – and said, 'Here you are,' as though nothing had happened.

Taiji glared at the new omelette sandwiches and pumpkin soup that had been placed in front of him. 'But this is just the same as before,' he said, his voice sharp with annoyance. He had told Kai clearly that the meal wasn't right.

'It isn't the same,' said Kai.

'What do you mean?'

'Try the sandwiches and you will see. I believe this may be your true remembrance meal,' Kai said with a quiet assurance. Taiji didn't understand: how could Kai say that when he'd just served more of the same? Maybe he thought Taiji could be fooled because he was only a kid, but the look on Kai's face was sincere.

'*Miaow*,' Chibi mewed. It felt to Taiji as if the kitten was encouraging him to trust Kai. Kotoko had told Taiji she'd spoken to her dead brother at the restaurant. Taiji had known her for as long as he could remember and she wasn't the sort of person who told lies. He had trusted her enough to come this far, so why lose faith now?

He turned again to the fresh sandwiches on the table. No matter how closely he scrutinised them, he couldn't see any difference from the previous ones. But he decided to try them anyway.

'Itadakimasu,' he muttered, picking one up, and then he gave a small gasp of surprise. The bread felt denser and springier than last time.

'What have you done differently?'

Taiji looked up at Kai, waiting for an explanation, but he just said, 'Please, go ahead while they're still warm.'

Taiji thought that perhaps he would only understand once he started eating. So he nodded and took a bite. The moment he tasted it, he knew. This was the sandwich he had had that day, the sandwich Fumika had given him. Her words echoed in his ears.

Aren't you going to eat? . . . You can have one, if you want. I think they turned out pretty well!

Taiji felt tears welling up but he didn't want to cry in front of Kai. He put the sandwich down on the plate and rubbed his eyes fiercely on his sleeve. When he looked up again, his vision was blurry.

What's happening . . .? At first he thought he'd rubbed his eyes too hard. He blinked a few times but the haze didn't clear. Taiji looked round and realised that the room seemed different. The whole restaurant was wrapped in mist – it was like being inside a cloud. Kai, who had been standing beside the table, was gone, and Taiji could no longer hear the sound of the waves, the cries of the gulls, or the tick-tock of the clock. He noticed that its pendulum had stopped.

It wasn't the strangeness of it all that bothered him so much as the feeling that he had been left entirely alone. *What do I do now?* he panicked. Then he heard a mew from down by his feet.

Taiji was relieved to see that Chibi was right there, peering up at him – so he wasn't alone. There was something odd about the kitten's mewing, though. It almost sounded muted.

'Hey, your voice has gone weird,' he said to Chibi, before realising with surprise that his own voice was just as muffled.

'What's happening?' Taiji whispered, reaching into his pocket to check his phone. Maybe there would be something on the news or social media that could explain what was going on. But the phone's screen was dark and it wouldn't switch on even when Taiji pressed the power button. Cut off from the rest of the world, he felt even more helpless than before. He looked down at Chibi as though the little cat might be able to offer some form of explanation.

But Chibi seemed unperturbed. '*Miaow,*' he mewed, trotting towards the door as if he wanted to go out.

Taiji looked through the window and saw that the whiteness was even thicker outside. It looked less like mist and more like the kind of smoke that billows off dry ice. He didn't think it would be a good idea to go out there.

'Don't, it's dangerous!' he called out and he was just about to dash after Chibi when it happened: the door opened with a clinking sound and a small figure entered. A girl.

Chibi greeted her with a '*miaow*'. So that was why he'd gone to the door.

'Thanks,' the girl replied. Her voice was also muffled, but even so Taiji recognised it. He recognised her face too. He knew who she was the moment she entered the room.

Words came to his mind – *It's really you, I've wanted to see you for ages* – but he was too shocked to speak. He believed in miracles, but now that one was actually happening, he was frozen to his chair.

Fumika Nakazato had appeared in the Chibineko Kitchen.

'Hello again, Taiji,' she said.

She looked a little out of focus, but she was the real Fumika. 'Thanks for coming to visit me,' she said.

Taiji remained silent. Having come all this way hoping to speak to her, now he didn't feel ready.

'*Miaow*,' Chibi mewed in encouragement before making his way back to the rocking chair.

'Can I sit down?' Fumika asked. She had come over to stand by the empty place opposite him.

'Y . . . Yes, of course. That seat is for you, Fumika,' Taiji managed to say. His throat had gone dry and he was struggling to speak properly.

'You ordered the food for me, didn't you, Taiji?' she said.

'I suppose I did . . .'

'Thank you.'

Fumika pulled out her chair and sat down. She looked at the omelette sandwiches and the thick pumpkin soup. 'Let's eat before it gets cold.'

Taiji picked up the sandwich again and took another bite. It was still warm, and it smelled and tasted as delicious as before – the generous layer of butter had probably helped seal in the flavour.

Taiji suddenly felt Fumika's eyes on him. She hadn't touched her food though she'd been the one who suggested they start. She was just sitting there quietly.

'Aren't you going to eat?' Taiji asked her, puzzled.

'I am eating,' she said.

'What?'

'The steam is my food.'

'What do you mean?'

'Well, I suppose it's the smell really, not the steam. When you die, you can't *actually* eat anything from this world any more,' Fumika said. 'That's why we light incense sticks at the butsudan and at graves, you know. The scented smoke is food for the dead.'

'Really?' Taiji had never heard anything like this before.

'And that's why I can only stay here while the food is still steaming,' Fumika continued.

'You mean, you're going to disappear?'

'Not disappear exactly. But go back to the other world.'

So their time together was limited. 'Can I see you again?' asked Taiji.

'I don't think so. Taiji . . . this is probably the last time we can meet.'

'The last time?'

Shocked, Taiji turned back to his remembrance meal which was getting steadily cooler. The days were still mild but it was almost November now, after all. Time was passing quickly. While he sat there dithering, Taiji's chance to apologise to Fumika was slipping away. This moment would soon be gone and he would never have another like it in his whole life. He didn't want to be weighed down by regret any more, so he spoke.

'That day at cram school, when you gave me the sandwich – I'm sorry I said those things about you.'

He had finally done it – he had managed to apologise. But there was still more he wanted to say to Fumika. Summoning up every ounce of courage he possessed, he made the first romantic confession of his life.

'What I said wasn't true. I don't hate you,' he said. He couldn't look Fumika in the eye. His voice came out in a squeak, and his heart was pounding so fast it was hard to breathe. But he persevered, finally putting into words the feelings he had held on to for so long.

'I really, really like you. I always have, Fumika.'

I like you more than anyone. I love you.

He had managed to tell her how he felt. Now he just had to listen to her reply. Taiji raised his eyes timidly and looked at Fumika.

She was crying.

'Sorry, I didn't mean to cry . . . It's OK. You don't need to apologise, or look so worried, Taiji. It's my turn now, so please just listen to what I have to say.

'That day at cram school, when you said you hated me, I was so, so shocked. I hid it for the rest of the day, but when I got home I cried, *really* cried. My mum thought it was to do with my illness and I didn't want to worry her, so I told her the truth. I told her I was sad because you said you hated me.'

Fumika paused. Her eyes were wet but she had stopped crying. She looked straight at Taiji.

'But my mum laughed and told me I had got it wrong, that you probably didn't hate me at all. She said, *I wonder if, maybe, Taiji really likes you.* And that made me really, really happy.

'I mean, I knew I wasn't going to live a long time. The doctors never said that to me but you can just tell. So I might never get the chance to fall in love with someone, or to have someone fall in love with me. I didn't know how many years I had left and sometimes I felt like there was no point in me being born at all. I even thought about ending my life before the illness got worse and I became more of a burden to my parents.

'But before that I wanted to go to school, even just once. I wanted to learn with other kids, eat lunch with them and just live a normal life for a while. I wanted friends, too, though I wasn't sure if it would be possible. I couldn't go to primary school in the end but I did get to go to cram school. Then I met you, Taiji. And, well . . . OK, I'll tell you, seeing as this is my only chance.

'Taiji – I really liked you. You were the first person I ever fell in love with. You were so clever and kind and cool. When my mum told me that you might actually like me too, I was so happy! I decided to give you chocolates next Valentine's Day and tell you how I felt. But before I could tell you, my chest got really painful and I collapsed. They took me away in an ambulance and I died. It's so silly, isn't it? Especially when we both felt the same way about each other.'

Tears began to spill from Taiji's eyes. The time he had left with Fumika seemed unbearably precious, and unbearably sad.

Taiji's tears weren't so much for himself as for Fumika. He was still alive, after all. It must be far more painful for her than it was for him. He tried to pull himself together, wiping his eyes roughly with the back of his hand. *Don't cry, don't cry, don't cry*, he told himself. He wanted to offer Fumika some words of comfort – to tell her how glad he was that at least now, they both knew how the other felt. But Fumika spoke first.

'Hey – this is a date, isn't it? We're on a date, Taiji!'

Taiji nodded, feeling as though his chest would break open with the sadness. This was their first and last date. Once the steam stopped rising from the pumpkin soup, Fumika would disappear from this world. They only had a few minutes left and he didn't want to waste them.

Fumika must have been thinking the same thing. She waited for Taiji to dry his tears and then, as though starting afresh, she asked: 'Hey, Taiji. What do you want to be when you grow up?'

'I . . . I want to be a doctor,' Taiji told her. That was why he was taking the junior high school entrance exams – so that when he finished school, he could get into a national university to study medicine. He had never told anyone about this goal before, not his parents or his cram-school teacher. He didn't want people to make fun of him or tell him it was impossible. It was better to keep ambitions like that to yourself. But Taiji thought Fumika would understand and he wanted to share his dream with her.

Fumika didn't laugh. 'I know you can do it, Taiji,' she said, nodding earnestly. 'You'll become a doctor and help people who are sick and in pain, won't you?'

'Yes, I will,' Taiji replied. She had understood perfectly. He wanted to cure lots of people who were ill. As he nodded, he suddenly thought, *If I'd been born ten, no, twenty years earlier, maybe I could have made Fumika better. Except, if I'd been born earlier, I would never have fallen in love with her. But that would be OK . . .*

If there were a god, and that god had told Taiji that he had to make a decision, he would choose to be born twenty years earlier, without hesitation. He would have done anything to save Fumika.

Thinking of this, tears welled up in his eyes all over again. Then from over on the rocking chair there came a '*miaow*'. *This is not the moment for tears!* Chibi seemed to be saying. Taiji looked down and saw that the pumpkin soup was almost cold. Their time was coming to an end.

Gazing at the steam as it dwindled away, Fumika said, 'Can I tell you what my dream for the future was?

I wanted to get married and be a kind mum. Like *my* mum.'

Taiji imagined Fumika – a grown-up Fumika – beaming as she made omelette sandwiches for her children. 'But now that can never happen,' she said. For Fumika, time had stopped; she would always be primary-school aged. The image of a grown-up Fumika slowly faded from Taiji's mind. It was a dream that could never come true.

'So,' Fumika continued, 'now you need to focus on making *your* dreams a reality. OK?'

OK, Taiji began to say – but before he could, she had faded away. Panicking, he reached out to touch the mug of pumpkin soup. It was stone cold. Then he heard Fumika's parting words, carried through the haze.

'I have to go now. Thank you for coming to see me, Taiji. Bye bye.'

Though he could no longer see her, somehow he knew that she was waving to him. His heart was breaking but he gritted his teeth, forced a smile and waved in the direction of Fumika's voice.

'Goodbye,' he said. He had done it – he had said his farewell to Fumika, the first girl he had ever loved.

Chibi jumped down from the rocking chair and darted towards the door. He mewed towards something Taiji couldn't see, saying his own goodbye. The bell clinked as the door opened and then closed again. For a while the boy and the little cat just sat there, gazing at it.

Fumika was gone. Taiji didn't know where – only that it was somewhere far beyond his reach.

The world returned to normal. The morning mist cleared and the old clock resumed its ticking. The sound of the waves floated in along with the cries of the seagulls. Chibi returned to his place on the rocking chair. Taiji touched his cheek, only to find it was dry. After all that crying, his tears hadn't even left a trace. Had he dreamt it all?

Dream or no dream, he was glad he had seen Fumika. Opposite him on the table were her omelette sandwiches and pumpkin soup – her remembrance meal. The food was untouched.

Suddenly Kai reappeared, coming over to put a teacup down on the table.

'Some green tea for you.' He bowed and was just turning back to the kitchen when Taiji said, 'I spoke to Fumika.'

'I see,' said Kai without a hint of surprise. This must be a place where miracles were expected.

'Could I ask you something?' said Taiji.

'Certainly. Whatever you like.'

Taiji thought about asking why it was that dead people could visit this place, but he had a feeling Kai would just say he didn't know. And it didn't matter – not now he'd met Fumika. Something else was troubling him.

'What was the difference between the sandwiches?' He still couldn't work it out. Only the second batch had tasted exactly right and had brought Fumika to the restaurant.

Kai answered Taiji's question simply. 'It was the bread.'

'The bread?'

'Yes. I made the first loaf using normal wheat flour, but the second was gluten-free.'

Taiji had seen 'gluten-free' before on labels in convenience stores and at the supermarket. He understood about wheat allergies; there were people in his family and in his class who suffered from them.

'The bread in Miss Nakazato's sandwich was made with rice flour,' Kai continued.

But Taiji was still confused. Something was missing from Kai's explanation. If he himself hadn't realised

Fumika's sandwiches were made with rice bread, how could Kai possibly have known when he hadn't tried them?

When Taiji asked him this, Kai replied, 'I spoke with Ms Niki on the telephone.' Kotoko had clearly told Kai more than just Taiji's name, but he was still puzzled.

'How did Kotoko know it was rice bread?' asked Taiji. Surely that was impossible – unless Kotoko and Fumika already knew each other, and he was unaware?

'I don't believe Ms Niki knew,' said Kai.

'Then how . . .?'

'It was the cookie.'

'What?' said Taiji.

'Ms Niki told me about the incident with the cookie.'

'You mean . . . So that's why . . .?'

'Yes, precisely. Miss Nakazato couldn't eat the cookie because it contained wheat flour,' said Kai.

Taiji remembered the way Fumika had screwed up her face and begun to say something, and how he had run off without waiting to hear what it was. And then he'd been horrible about her. It was Taiji who had got it all wrong.

'It was only a guess, of course. There could have been another explanation,' Kai went on. That was why he had made the sandwich with ordinary bread first of all. But when Fumika failed to appear, he had known exactly what to try next.

Everything made sense now. If Taiji had just kept as level-headed as Kai maybe he would never have hurt Fumika.

'Please take your time,' Kai said, bowing his head and returning to the kitchen.

Taiji stared down at the table, biting his lip. He heard Chibi mew but he didn't look up. All he could think about was the girl who was gone. Memories fade over time but he knew he would never forget Fumika. She was his first love, and you can only have one of those in your lifetime.

A special recipe from the Chibineko Kitchen

Easy Omelette Sandwich

Ingredients (serves 1)

- 2 eggs
- 1 tbsp mayonnaise
- 1 tsp shiro dashi liquid
- 1 tsp water
- 2 slices thick white bread

Method

1. Put the mayonnaise, shiro dashi and water in a small bowl and mix well.
2. Beat the eggs in a separate bowl.
3. Combine the eggs and the mayonnaise mixture, and pour into a microwavable container (ideally a square one about the same size as the bread).

4. Cover with cling film and microwave for 1 minute. Continue to microwave for 30-second bursts until the eggs fluff up and the omelette is cooked to your liking. (You can lift it and check underneath to make sure it is done.)
5. Toast the bread and then sandwich the omelette between the slices.

Tips

You can also spread the toast with butter or mustard before filling the sandwich.

3

A grey tabby and a bowl of peanut rice

落花生
Peanuts

A speciality of Chiba Prefecture, where approximately 80 per cent of the peanuts grown in Japan are produced. Peanut Day is celebrated on 11 November when the peanuts are said to be at their best.

One popular local product is peanut monaka: peanut-shaped wafer shells with a filling of sweet bean paste and peanut. They can be bought at Nagomi Yoneya's sweet-shop and at station kiosks, along with other sweet snacks like Orandaya's peanut dacquoise and peanut pies.

Though a month had passed, Kotoko often thought of the day she had visited the Chibineko Kitchen. She recalled how she had set out for the restaurant in despair and how everything had changed when Yuito appeared, summoned by the food Kai had cooked. And she remembered what her brother had said to her, before fading away.

I have just one favour to ask you . . . I want you to perform on stage.

At first she hadn't understood, but Kai had helped her to tease out Yuito's meaning.

I wonder if, perhaps, your brother wishes to take to the stage once more himself.

After she left the Chibineko Kitchen Kotoko went straight to Kumagai and asked him to let her join his theatre company. She wanted to follow in her brother's footsteps and take on speaking roles, rather than bit parts as before.

It felt almost as though Kumagai had been waiting for Kotoko to approach him. His response was stern but not unkind: 'You're welcome to come to training but whether you make it as an actor is up to you, Kotoko. You'll have to work hard to be cast in main roles.'

She looked him in the eye as she thanked him and, just like that, she became an official member of the troupe. It was hard going at first as Kotoko had no stamina and didn't know how to project her voice. During training Kumagai often yelled at her; sometimes she ended up slumped on the floor, completely exhausted, but she never gave up. Little by little, she could feel herself making progress, and when things were particularly tough, she thought of Yuito watching over her, and of Kai's words.

The very best of luck. Chibi and I will be with you all the way.

When she wasn't rehearsing with the group, she went to the gym to build up her stamina and did vocal exercises in the park, reciting 'The Medicine Peddler' speech over and over again.

A month passed and the date of her first production was approaching. She had been given a speaking role – perhaps because it was only a small company. When Kotoko told her parents about the play, their faces brightened for the first time since Yuito's death. They had a barrage of questions for her. What was the play about? Did she have many lines? Would she be in costume? Who else would be performing?

'Well, we'll have to come along to support you,' said Kotoko's father.

'Absolutely! I can't wait,' her mother chimed in.

They pressed money for the tickets into her hands then and there. She could see that they had needed something like this to bring them back to life. Or maybe it was their daughter's recovery they'd been patiently waiting for. She had been broken by her brother's death, tormenting herself for months on end with the thought that she should have been the one to die. But now things were getting better.

'I'll put the tickets on the butsudan,' Kotoko said, and her mother and father smiled and nodded, tears welling in their eyes.

'Your brother will be so proud,' her father said quietly. The three of them knelt in front of the butsudan, palms pressed together, and shared Kotoko's news with Yuito. Speaking about him and saying his name was no longer quite as painful.

Later that day, Kotoko scoured the department-store food halls for fat greenling. She cooked it the way Yuito always had, simmering the fish with plenty of saké and ginger and then adding soy sauce and sugar. When the greenling was ready she used the leftover sauce to make nikogori and prepared fluffy rice in an earthenware pot. She laid everything out on a tray and carried it over to the table where she set out portions for her parents, herself and her brother. She wasn't as good a cook as Kai, but this was a kagezen nonetheless – her own version. As the family ate, they shared memories of Yuito. Kotoko and her parents talked and talked late into the night, and as they talked, they cried – but they were fond tears.

Yuito did not appear to them, neither did they hear his voice. *This visit, today, will be my only visit to this world*, he had said to Kotoko at the Chibineko Kitchen. Nothing would bring him back now. But they could finally see a way to carry on without him.

It was all thanks to Kai Fukuchi, thought Kotoko. His cooking, his words, had been what she needed to get back on her feet. She wanted to repay his kindness and decided to invite him to her play.

They had only spoken once since her visit to the Chibineko Kitchen, when she had phoned Kai to tell him about Taiji, guessing that the young boy might set out for the little restaurant by the sea on his own.

'This is the Chibineko Kitchen. Thank you for your call.' His voice was just as gentle as she remembered. Chibi mewed in the background and Kotoko could almost make out the sound of waves breaking and the cries of the black-tailed gulls. She pictured Kai and the little kitten in that wood-panelled room as she spoke, explaining Taiji's situation.

'I see,' Kai replied when Kotoko had finished. 'Taiji Hashimoto. We'll make the arrangements. Thank you very much for calling.'

The conversation had ended there, but Kotoko wanted to see Kai again.

Catching up with Kumagai after rehearsals one day, Kotoko told him that she planned to invite Kai to the play.

He didn't know who she meant at first. 'Kai Fukuchi? Who's that again?'

'You know, from the Chibineko Kitchen.'

Kumagai looked up as though searching his memory before nodding. 'Oh yes, the owner's son.'

'The owner . . .?'

'Nanami, Kai's mother. She's in her fifties or thereabouts – I told you about her before, I think. You didn't meet her, then?'

Kotoko had completely forgotten that she had gone to the Chibineko Kitchen expecting to see Nanami; her meeting with Yuito had driven it out of her mind.

'No, I didn't. When I went there was no sign of anyone but Kai – and the little cat, of course.'

'Oh, well it's Nanami who writes the blog. She explains why she opened the Chibineko Kitchen – you can read it for yourself,' said Kumagai. 'I haven't looked at it for a while . . .'

As soon as Kotoko got home, she searched for the blog and found it straight away. It was titled 'Remembrance Meals at the Chibineko Kitchen', and there were a lot of posts, accompanied by photos of the sea, the black-tailed gulls and the restaurant. There was a photo of Chibi, too, sitting by the chalkboard, looking even smaller than when Kotoko had visited.

Kotoko ran her eye over the posts, looking for one that would tell her how the restaurant had come to be in existence. Then she noticed something and her breath caught in her throat. The most recent entry was more than two months old. After what looked like years of almost weekly updates, the posts had stopped abruptly.

Kotoko was suddenly uneasy. Something must have happened. Feeling a sense of helplessness she phoned the Chibineko Kitchen, wanting to hear Kai's voice. But he didn't answer. The phone rang and rang until

Kotoko hung up, her anxiety mounting. *What should I do?* Her indecision was momentary: *I'll go there*, she resolved. It was only mid-afternoon and if she set off immediately, she could be at the restaurant before it got dark. She let her parents know she was leaving and dashed out of the door.

At Tokyo station Kotoko boarded the first-class carriage of a Sobu Line rapid train. Slipping into one of the few empty seats, she got out her phone to read the blog, starting at the very beginning.

The first post was headed 'My First Remembrance Meals'. In it, Nanami wrote that her husband – Kai's father – had been a fisherman until their son was born, when he took a job at the local steelworks. Times had changed and it was becoming difficult to make a living in fishing, but Nanami's husband loved the sea and couldn't leave it behind completely. He still had his little boat and a boat permit, and on days off from the steelworks he would go out to fish. One day he had set out early in the morning, telling his wife he'd bring something back for dinner. But he had never returned.

'He's still somewhere out at sea,' Nanami had written. Twenty years had passed since that day, without her knowing whether he was alive or dead.

Nanami, now raising Kai alone, had to find a way to support herself and her son. They had some savings from her husband's wages, and Nanami had some money of her own: she had inherited a plot of land that had been in the family for generations and which she was able to sell off for a good price thanks to the construction of the nearby Aqua-Line motorway that crossed Tokyo Bay. With that money she renovated their house and opened the Chibineko Kitchen.

There, as well as cooking meals for customers, she began to make kagezen to pray for her husband's safety. Soon, she wrote, customers began requesting remembrance meals themselves and reporting that their loved ones had appeared to them. Nanami's longing for her missing husband seemed to have brought about this miracle.

But, of course, it was Kai who had prepared Kotoko's remembrance meal, not Nanami. She wondered if Kai too thought of his long-lost father whenever he was cooking.

Kotoko scrolled to a more recent blog post.

'My son is taking care of the restaurant while I'm in hospital.' So that explained Nanami's absence at the Chibineko Kitchen. Perhaps when Kai cooked kagezen, it was his mother's health he was praying for.

The question remained, where was Nanami now? Kotoko was still scanning the blog for clues when the train pulled in to the station. Out on the platform, she saw that the sun was already setting. The Chibineko Kitchen was only open for breakfast. *Maybe there'll be no one there*, thought Kotoko – but she didn't turn back. Instead, she hurried out of the deserted station and into a taxi, impatient to get there as fast as she could.

The taxi sped along the quiet roads and in less than fifteen minutes they had reached the beach. The November days were short and the last of the daylight had faded, but a bright moon lit up the sand. The only sound Kotoko could hear was the lapping of the waves, but no seabirds crying, no owls hooting or night herons squawking: it was as though every living thing was asleep. As she hurried up the path, the seashells seemed to crunch particularly noisily beneath her feet.

The restaurant soon came into view. None of its windows were lit. This should have come as no surprise, but Kotoko's heart sank nonetheless. *What if Kai and Chibi have gone for ever?* Kotoko thought of her brother and of the girl who had been Taiji's first love. No matter how much you cared about someone, you always had to say goodbye in the end. A wave of panic swept over her. But then she heard the gentle sound of a bell.

Clink, clink. The door of the Chibineko Kitchen opened and Kotoko saw someone emerge into the moonlight. It was Kai. She thought he looked slightly different and then realised that he wasn't wearing his glasses. The bell clinked again as he closed the door behind him and locked up. He had just turned round and was about to set off along the beach when he caught sight of Kotoko.

'Ms Niki?' he said, surprised to see her at this hour. Kotoko was momentarily lost for words. She really had believed he was gone for good.

'G . . . Good evening,' she stammered.

'Good evening,' Kai replied. He seemed thrown, too.

Kotoko could bear the silence no longer and blurted out, 'I read your mother's blog.' Then she stopped, unsure how to go on. This was only the second time they had met; she didn't know Kai well enough to ask about his mother's illness but she couldn't take the words back, so she remained quiet, waiting for him to speak.

'I see,' he said at last. 'Her funeral was last week.' His voice was low and betrayed no hint of emotion.

Somehow, Kotoko had been expecting this, but even so she didn't know what to say.

'If you are here for a meal, I am very sorry to disappoint you, but I have decided to close the Chibineko Kitchen. I'm leaving town,' explained Kai. 'Now that my mother is gone, I no longer have any reason to make kagezen.'

So Kotoko had been right. Kai had kept the restaurant open while his mother was in hospital to offer food in prayer for her safe return.

Losing the woman who had brought him up single-handedly must be devastating for him. Kotoko's hand went to her chest. After Yuito had died, it had felt as though there was a hollow where her heart should be. Perhaps it was the same for Kai now.

'And now, I'm afraid you'll have to excuse me. I am on my way to serve one last kagezen meal.' Kai bowed to Kotoko. She watched as he began to walk up the path, his figure growing smaller and smaller, as if he were already miles away.

She didn't want to let him go off on his own like this. Before she knew what she was doing, she had called after him, 'Can I come with you?' Her cheeks grew hot. Turning up at the closed restaurant and now this – she was acting like one of those women who barges uninvited into the home of their intended and makes themselves comfortable.

Kai stopped and turned. He was silhouetted by the moonlight and Kotoko couldn't make out his expression but she heard him say quietly, 'If you like. Please, feel free to accompany me.'

Kai led the way along the dark seashore. He was empty-handed. If he was going to prepare a kagezen, why hadn't he brought ingredients and cooking utensils? Kotoko wondered. She wanted to ask who he was cooking for so late in the evening, and where he would go after closing the Chibineko Kitchen. But she kept her questions to herself, sensing that if she followed him, everything might become clear. Kai offered no explanations and they walked to the end of the beach in silence.

They reached the deserted road lit by the moon rather than the bright street lamps Kotoko was used to in Tokyo. The houses were in darkness too. They couldn't all be empty, surely, yet Kotoko heard no voices, no sound of televisions.

They followed a riverside footpath lined with cherry

trees. This was a spot famous for its beauty, especially when the trees were in bloom – 720 of them, according to the town's official website. Over the changing seasons, flowers carpeted the riverbank too: hydrangeas, cosmos and rapeseed, the official flower of Chiba Prefecture. The trees were naked of blossom now as it was November, but the bridge over the Koitogawa was illuminated, and the reflection on the glassy water made it look as though there were another town lying at the bottom of the river.

After a short while, Kai turned off the footpath onto a narrow side road. As they left the river behind, Kotoko realised she had no idea where they were, but, strangely, she wasn't nervous – part of her wanted to go on walking close behind Kai for ever.

Before long he stopped.

'That's where I will be making the kagezen,' he said, pointing to an old weathered house with a traditional tiled roof and overhanging eaves. The adjoining plot of land looked as though it was being farmed, but in the darkness Kotoko couldn't make out what was growing in the field.

'Peanuts,' Kai suddenly said, as though reading her thoughts.

*

The Japanese peanut industry was now on the wane. More and more peanuts were being imported cheaply from abroad and the amount of land given over to peanut farming in Chiba Prefecture was dwindling. The man they were about to visit, Yoshio Kurata, was the only son of a peanut-farming family, Kai told Kotoko. He had turned eighty-two this year. Long ago, before the Tokyo Olympics in the 1960s, the peanuts produced by Yoshio's family were considered the most delicious for miles around. Bakeries and restaurants queued up to buy them by the crateful, but Yoshio didn't take over the family business.

'You don't want to become a peanut farmer. Far better to join a company and earn a salary,' his father had said. It was difficult to go against your parents' wishes in those days, so when Yoshio finished junior high school he found work straight away, first at a local building firm, then at a car repair workshop and finally at the new steelworks. Built on land reclaimed from the sea, the works had opened in 1965 and was run by one of the largest corporations in Japan.

Just as Yoshio's father had predicted, the family's peanut business began to fail: as hard as he and his wife laboured in the fields, they were unable to compete with the cheap imports. When he was about thirty,

Yoshio's parents sold off most of their farmland, keeping only one field next to the house where they grew peanuts just for themselves.

The years went by and Yoshio met and married a woman named Setsu, four years his junior. Getting married in your thirties was considered late in those days, and his mother and father were delighted; their daughter-in-law brought some youthfulness back into the house. Setsu began to work in the field with Yoshio's parents, Yoshio joining them on his days off, and every year they harvested the peanuts and ate them together as a family.

'Well, what do you think? Good, aren't they?' Yoshio's father once said proudly.

'They're so delicious, it almost seems a shame to eat them,' Setsu replied, causing her parents-in-law to burst out laughing at the absurdity of this answer.

Yoshio wished those days could have gone on for ever. But less than ten years later, his parents fell ill in quick succession. After several years of being confined to bed, his father passed away, followed soon after by his mother. When it was just the two of them left in the house, Yoshio had bowed his head to Setsu: 'I'm sorry.' He hadn't noticed the passage of time but somehow they were both now in their late forties. The years had flown by and here they were with no children. Yoshio wasn't sure whether he was apologising for that, or for the fact that Setsu had had to look after his parents as they neared the end. But his wife didn't ask him to explain, saying gently, 'It's all right.'

The conversation ended there that day. Afterwards Yoshio wished that they had talked about it properly.

The years continued to pass swiftly. Yoshio turned sixty and retired from work – not yet an old man but certainly not a young one either. Half his life was already behind him, and both his and Setsu's hair had turned completely grey. The couple lived on Yoshio's pension from the steelworks and poured their energy into working the field beside their house. It had been Setsu's idea: 'Surely even a couple of old fossils like us can grow enough food to live on,' she had said, jokingly. But in fact that really was all they could manage to produce. When Yoshio looked around, he saw a world he hardly recognised. Every other peanut farmer had sold up their land and gone elsewhere. Their friends had all either moved house, gone into retirement homes or passed away. The neighbourhood was scattered with empty houses. But he wasn't lonely – not with Setsu by his side.

Together they went to the supermarket and to the library. They worked up a sweat side by side in the field and enjoyed going out for a meal once a week. They went on holiday, too, though never very far away. It was a full life.

'Well – let's hope next year is as uneventful as this one,' they would say to each other as they neared the end of each year. *Please, just give me a little longer with Setsu. That's all I ask for*, Yoshio would pray before the butsudan or when visiting a shrine. And for some years the gods and buddhas granted him his wish.

The end came abruptly. Setsu fell ill and soon after drew her last breath. Yoshio held his wife's funeral as December drew to a close and saw in the new year alone. He stopped visiting the library and going out for meals but he still tended his garden and harvested peanuts from the field. They tasted just as they had when Setsu and his parents were alive. That, at least, would never change.

Yoshio had been living this way for about a year when one day, as he worked in the garden, he had a stabbing pain in his back. It didn't feel like a strained muscle and he had a strong sense of foreboding. When he went to hospital for a consultation, he was told that cancer had spread throughout his body. 'I'm afraid it will be difficult to treat,' said a doctor young enough to be his grandchild.

'It was the same for my mother,' said Kai. Now Kotoko understood why Nanami had been in hospital. She wanted to say something but couldn't find the right words. 'Mr Kurata was in the same ward as her,' Kai added.

The word 'was' caught Kotoko's attention. 'You mean he's out of hospital now?'

'For the moment, yes,' Kai replied. 'He told the doctors that he wanted to deal with his house and the plot of land while he could still get around by himself.'

'Is he well enough for that?' Kotoko feared for Yoshio, all alone in this little house on the edge of town.

'It was Mr Kurata's decision,' Kai said. Perhaps, with no family nearby, he had had no choice but to handle everything by himself – even his own funeral arrangements.

'He will be going back into hospital tomorrow,' Kai continued. He seemed to know every detail of the situation and Kotoko wondered just how long he had known Yoshio. Reading her thoughts once again, Kai explained, 'He was a regular at the restaurant.' So it was to the Chibineko Kitchen that Yoshio and Setsu had gone for their weekly meal out.

'Mr Kurata stopped coming after his wife's death but I met him again when I went to see my mother in hospital.' That was when Yoshio had asked Kai for a remembrance meal.

It was late to be calling on someone at home but Yoshio had told Kai he would be busy during the day, making arrangements. 'He has decided to have his house demolished, and to sell the land,' Kai said. Yoshio was erasing all traces of his life.

'Shall we?' said Kai, leading Kotoko along the edge of the field.

'There are no lights on . . .' she said.

The house was dark and utterly silent. Was Yoshio sleeping or had he deteriorated and ended up being admitted to hospital early? Kai didn't seem concerned. He just murmured, seemingly out of nowhere, 'It's a saucer moon tonight.'

Kotoko looked up to see a thin crescent moon the shape of an upturned dish in the night sky and wondered what had made Kai mention it. Meanwhile he was heading purposefully round the back of the house, seeming to know exactly where to go. They emerged into a large, traditional garden with a persimmon tree, a plum tree and a neat but empty flower-bed. On the raised veranda sat an old man, pale-faced and as skinny as a withered tree. This must be Yoshio Kurata.

'Good evening,' Kai said, bowing.

'I was sorry I couldn't be at your mother's funeral,' Yoshio said brusquely without returning Kai's greeting, his voice hoarse.

'That's all right. Please, don't worry,' Kai replied matter-of-factly, as though he didn't want to dwell on the funeral. 'This is Ms Kotoko Niki,' he said, and Yoshio nodded in Kotoko's direction. 'Now, may I get set up in the kitchen?'

'Yes, use whatever you need,' said Yoshio.

Kai thanked him and took off his shoes before stepping up onto the veranda and into the house.

Kotoko stood lost in thought, watching him go, until Yoshio said, 'Shouldn't you be going with him?'

Perhaps he thought she'd been taken on by the Chibineko Kitchen. This wasn't strictly true, but she had come here to support Kai. She should definitely go inside and help.

'May I?' she asked.

'Course you can,' said Yoshio.

Kotoko stepped out of her shoes and up into a chilly passageway. The sliding doors to the veranda had been left wide open and shafts of moonlight spilled in so that she could make out Kai disappearing down the corridor. Kotoko heard the click of a switch and then light pooled out from the doorway ahead of her. Catching up with Kai, she found herself in an old-fashioned kitchen: there was no microwave or hot-water dispenser, just a small fridge and an ancient-looking gas hob. But the place was spotless and the pots and pans had been polished until they gleamed.

'I'll start on the rice,' Kai said, placing an earthenware pot on the hob. The ingredients and cooking utensils were already set out neatly on a worktop: Kai must have brought them along earlier. Now Kotoko understood why he had come empty-handed.

'What are you going to cook?' she asked.

'Peanut rice.' Yoshio's remembrance meal.

The Japanese word for peanut, 'rakkasei', comes from its Chinese name which means 'born when the flowers fall'. Once a peanut plant has flowered, the petals drop and the stems droop downwards, bury themselves in the soil and begin to grow into peanuts.

'These come from the plot next to the house,' Kai told Kotoko, taking handfuls of the peanuts from a vegetable basket, dry earth still clinging to their shells. 'Harvesting them is a lot of work. You dig up the plants, gather them in bundles and stand them with their roots in the air for a week.' He went on to explain that the next stage is to pick up the peanut shells and shake them; if they rattle, the nuts are ready for the final stage of drying, piled in mounds out in the fields.

Yoshio couldn't have been strong enough for the task this year; Kai must have harvested these peanuts himself. He didn't mention this, however, but instead told Kotoko that the nuts come into season towards the end of the year: 'The 11th of November was Peanut Day, so the new crop should be at their best now.'

Kai's hands were busy as he spoke, shelling the pale pink peanuts one by one and dropping them into a glass bowl. When it was full, he turned to Kotoko: 'Now all we need to do is cook them along with the rice, some salt and a dash of saké.'

'You don't need to soak the rice first?'

Kai shook his head. 'It's new rice.' The first crop of the year, freshly harvested, was always especially moist. Pointing to a wooden cupboard, he asked, 'Could I trouble you to fetch the salt?'

Kotoko opened it to find a row of ceramic jars. Despite looking old, there wasn't a speck of dust on them. There was a jar of pickled plums, a jar of sugar . . . She quickly found one filled with salt. As she handed it to Kai, her fingertips brushed his just for a second. Kai turned back to the stove as though nothing had happened.

'It's such a simple recipe you can hardly call it cooking,' he said, pouring the rice, water and peanuts into the earthenware pot and adding the salt and saké. He placed the lid on top and switched on the hob. 'It will take a little while to cook.'

Kai held Kotoko's gaze for a moment and she thought he was going to say something more, but then he looked away and quietly began to tidy up.

The sweet aroma of peanut rice permeated the kitchen. After twenty minutes had elapsed, Kai turned off the hob and set the rice aside to steam and become fluffy, before transferring a small helping into a bowl.

'Please, have a taste.'

Kotoko had eaten roasted peanuts before, but this was the first time she'd tried them boiled with rice. 'Itadakimasu,' she said, taking the bowl. The peanuts were soft, their sweetness, drawn out by the salt and saké, perfectly balanced by the simple flavour of the rice. It was as though Kotoko could taste the earth, see the fields. She had eaten only a mouthful, yet she felt a warmth spread through her body. This was what Kai's cooking did: it made people happy. She remembered that first taste of the fat greenling she had eaten at the Chibineko Kitchen.

'It's delicious,' she said. She was sure this dish, made with peanuts grown right here in his family's field, would bring about a miracle for Yoshio.

Kai placed the earthenware pot on a tray along with two rice bowls.

'Let's take Mr Kurata his meal.'

Yoshio was still sitting out on the veranda, gazing up at the moon. He didn't seem to notice Kai and Kotoko emerging from the house.

'Perhaps he's making a wish,' Kai murmured. 'People do say that when you wish on a saucer moon, it always comes true. Have you heard that? The moon catches your prayer, just as a dish collects water.'

Kotoko looked more closely at Yoshio. The expression on his upturned face was hard to read.

'Aren't you cold?' Kai asked the old man. 'Shall I set out your meal indoors?'

The November day had been mild, but the night was growing too chilly for someone elderly and sick to be lingering outside.

Yoshio shook his head. 'I'm fine. Feels better being out here than in a sickroom.' He was wearing a traditional quilted coat and he sat with a blanket on his lap. Kotoko could see that he was determined to stay where he was, looking out over the garden and the peanut field. She understood; the place must hold so many memories for him.

Kai didn't press him, but set down the tray, saying softly, 'Your peanut rice is ready.' He served some into a bowl and placed it on the veranda by Yoshio. Then he filled a second bowl. 'One for you and one for Mrs Kurata.'

Yoshio must have asked for a meal in memory of his late wife, yet he made no move to reach for the food or even to pick up his chopsticks. He just sat there, looking down at the two bowls.

'Will you not eat?' queried Kai.

Yoshio turned his pale face towards the younger man. 'I'm sorry. I know I asked you to make it but . . .'

Of course, Kotoko thought. *Why didn't I realise sooner?* Somebody whose body was riddled with cancer would struggle to swallow this kind of food. Kai frowned at

Yoshio's words, as though he too was reproaching himself.

'You'll have to forgive me. I knew I might not be able to eat it,' Yoshio continued. 'But I wanted to make an offering. One kagezen for my wife, Setsu, and one for me.'

'An offering?' said Kai.

'Yes. Consider this my funeral. I know I've not got long now.'

Neither Kotoko nor Kai knew what to say. Yoshio had no relatives to hold a service for him; he was extending a funeral invitation to his wife in the world beyond.

'The smell of those peanuts . . . They bring Setsu's face back to me so clearly. Thank you, both of you.'

Kotoko pictured the old lady she'd never met sitting by Yoshio's side, looking out at the plum tree and the garden that would soon be abandoned.

'I just wanted one last look at it all . . . to say farewell to the house,' Kotoko heard Yoshio say. She needed to get away.

Yoshio watched Kotoko retreat back inside. He felt guilty for not eating the food the young people had prepared so carefully. He had hoped to manage a mouthful or two but seeing Kai serve the peanut rice, a wave of grief had swept over him. *What's the point of living like this, alone in a world without Setsu? I've had enough now.*

He could still remember that cold winter's day as though it were yesterday – the day Setsu had died. It had begun when his wife, who never complained about anything, came to him bent over with her face twisted in pain. Fearing that she might have broken a bone, he took her to a small clinic nearby where the doctor, his expression sober, referred them to the hospital in the next town. After some tests, Setsu was given a diagnosis: 'I'm sorry to tell you this, Mrs Kurata, Mr Kurata . . .'

Yoshio's world went dark. He couldn't even remember leaving the hospital. But Setsu's words, when they got home again, remained etched in his memory: 'So, this is it, then.' It was as though she had known it was coming. Yoshio remained silent as Setsu went on: 'I'm sorry, love. You're going to have to look after me, just for a little while.'

No! Don't give up! Don't say 'just for a little while'! he had wanted to scream. Slowly, inexorably, the illness progressed, and there was nothing Yoshio could do to stop it. At first Setsu was in and out of hospital, and then she entered palliative care where the aim was to relieve the patients' pain rather than to cure them.

'I'm so grateful that it doesn't hurt,' she had murmured quietly from her hospital bed. Yoshio found himself unable to say anything, as usual.

'Thank you for yesterday, love,' Setsu said.

The previous day Yoshio had taken her out – their last date. At Mother Farm they had shared an ice cream, cold and sweet, and watched the children on school trips dashing about. After that they went to Hitomi Shrine, perched high on a hilltop overlooking the town. Standing before it, Yoshio pressed his palms together. *Please don't let Setsu feel any pain*, he prayed silently to the guardian god. He didn't ask for his wife to be well again – he knew that was impossible.

The next morning they rose early and took a taxi up Mount Kanozan, arriving at the Kujukutani viewpoint just before dawn. As the sun came up, it illuminated the sea of clouds that filled the valleys below. The surrounding hills rose out of the mist and faded away into the distance. The effect was breathtaking – just like an ink painting.

'I wonder if heaven is like this,' Setsu said. Yoshio couldn't bring himself to reply, but Setsu, gazing out over the glowing clouds, didn't seem to expect an answer. Seconds, minutes, maybe even an hour passed.

'Well, I suppose we'd better go,' Setsu said at last. The taxi drove them back down the winding mountain road and straight to the hospital. She wouldn't be coming home again.

Yoshio visited Setsu on the ward each morning. He was as quiet as ever; it was she who did all the talking, smiling at Yoshio and never complaining. 'I'm sorry I can't be the one taking care of you. But I'm so glad you'll be with me until the end . . .'

His wife was on strong pain medication and her sentences often tailed away. She spent less and less time awake each day. Yoshio would sit by Setsu as she slept, wanting just to be with her. *Please, give me a little more time*, he prayed to the gods.

But, far too soon, the moment came. Setsu had been comatose for several days; now she woke and spoke her final words. 'Yoshio, love, after I'm gone, I don't want you to grieve for me. You don't have to come to my grave or light incense for me. Just enjoy life for both of us – eat the things you like to eat, do the things you like to do. I'm so happy I got to spend my life with you . . .'

Setsu gave a faint smile and closed her eyes. A doctor came into the room, took her pulse, listened for her heartbeat, shone a light into her eyes and then turned to Yoshio, head bowed: 'Mr Kurata, I'm sorry for your loss.'

In that instant, memories of his wife flashed before Yoshio's eyes, the days the two of them had spent together unspooling in his mind like an old film.

A lifetime ago – a whole fifty years now – the pair had been introduced by an acquaintance acting as matchmaker. Yoshio had been taken with Setsu from the moment he saw her photograph.

The first time they met, Yoshio, fresh from a trip to the barbers, had worn a brand-new, navy-blue suit. When he saw Setsu, sitting in a flowery dress and looking a little shy, his breath caught. Later, he had steeled himself to ask, 'May I see you again?'

'Y . . . Yes,' Setsu had agreed, blushing.

They met more and more frequently, going to restaurants and taking long walks together. Just being with Setsu made Yoshio's heart race. One beautiful clear night they went to see the huge statue of the goddess Kannon that overlooked Tokyo Bay. As they walked back along the road beside the Koitogawa, Yoshio decided to tell Setsu how he felt. They were completely alone; the moon, a slender crescent like an upturned dish, was reflected in the dark river. Yoshio looked up at it and made a wish – that he and Setsu would be together always.

'Setsu, will you be my wife?' His words came out in a rush. Setsu was silent for a moment and then she burst out laughing. Yoshio's heart sank. *I've been such a fool*, he thought. He knew he wasn't a handsome man: his complexion was too tanned, his eyes too small, his nose too flat. What was he doing, proposing to the young and beautiful Setsu?

'I'm sorry,' Setsu said, interrupting Yoshio's train of thought. 'I'm just so happy, I can't help but laugh. I love you, Yoshio. Please marry me.'

Yoshio was lost for words. His vision blurred with tears.

'Or . . . you'd rather not?' Setsu peered at him, waiting for him to speak.

'No . . . I mean, yes! I would! Please marry me, Setsu!' At Yoshio's jumbled words, Setsu laughed again, then she took his hand and squeezed it.

And so they became husband and wife. The moon had granted Yoshio's wish.

Now Setsu was gone. *It'll be my turn next*, Yoshio had thought to himself at the crematorium as he completed the funeral rites, picking up fragments of Setsu's bones one by one with long chopsticks and placing them in the urn. And he was right. Yoshio soon fell ill with the same disease that had robbed him of his wife. Treatment wasn't possible, and he didn't have long to live.

By choice he would have spent his final weeks at home, but he didn't want to sully the house by dying in it, or leave someone else to have to deal with his body. So he resolved to go into hospital and wait quietly for the end, reminding himself that that was how it had been for Setsu and his parents too. 'It won't be so bad,' he tried to convince himself. 'It's where I was born, after all.' He'd arranged for the house to be demolished and the land sold, and for the proceeds to be given to the temple. He asked, too, that his remains be placed alongside the urns that held the bones of his family.

With all that done, he was left with just one regret. There was something he desperately wished he could have asked Setsu.

With a sigh, Yoshio dragged himself back to the present. Perhaps it was the medication he was taking, but more and more often now his mind would wander. Lost in thoughts of his wife, he had forgotten he was not alone. Kai stood beside him, and in front of him were the bowls of peanut rice, now stone cold. The night was wearing on and he had no reason to keep the two youngsters here. He was about to apologise again when he heard light footsteps – a woman's tread. For a moment Yoshio thought he would look up to see Setsu. But, of course, it was only the young woman, Kotoko. Steam spiralled upwards from the earthenware pot she was carrying.

'Ms Niki, what . . .?' said Kai, as confused as Yoshio.

'I'd like you to try this, Mr Kurata.'

'I already told you, I can't . . .' Yoshio started to say, irritated. And then the smell reached him: something salty, sour, so familiar. 'What is it?'

'Rice porridge with pickled plums,' she replied, and bowed her head. 'I helped myself to the jar of plums in your cupboard . . . I'm sorry.'

Setsu had always believed the old saying that a pickled plum a day keeps the doctor away. She had loved to pick the fruit from the tree in the garden and make shiraboshi-ume, plums pickled in salt, which could be stored for decades without going bad. Yoshio remembered each and every dish Setsu had made for him using these pickled plums. She had minced them with bonito flakes to make ume katsuo; she had mixed chopped pickled plum into rice along with dried baby sardines; and she'd made pork rolls with pickled plum and shiso leaves. Sometimes she'd even experimented with Western-style dishes: spaghetti with tuna, shiso and pickled plum, or pickled plum and cheese pizza toast.

The plums, simmered with saké and sugar, were delicious spread on top of crunchy toast, too. When Yoshio thanked Setsu for the jam she had made, she laughed and corrected him. 'It's not jam, it's umebishio! It's been around for hundreds of years – since the Edo period at least.'

And whenever Yoshio was laid up in bed with a winter cold, Setsu would serve him hot pickled-plum rice porridge. It was a dish he could always manage, even when he had no appetite.

'Allow me to serve you.'

Kai took the pot from Kotoko and lifted the lid. More steam wafted out and the tangy smell of pickled plum intensified. Yoshio's mouth, which had been bone-dry, began to water and his stomach rumbled.

'Here you are.' Kai dished a helping into a bowl and handed it to him. The pure-white rice porridge was marbled with the pink of the pickled plums.

As Yoshio took his first mouthful, a warmth spread through his body. The tartness of the fruit, blending with the subtle flavour of the rice, filled his mouth. The porridge was soft enough for him to swallow easily.

He noticed that Kai and Kotoko had laid out another floor cushion next to him on the veranda along with a second bowl of rice porridge. He knew they were for Setsu.

Yoshio polished off the contents of his bowl. 'Thank you . . .' he said and then stopped short. His voice sounded odd – strangely thick. He tried to clear his throat, but even that sound seemed muffled. Puzzled, he looked round, but his visitors were nowhere to be seen and, although it was night, the garden had suddenly filled with the type of haze you get in the mornings. All he could make out through the blanket of mist was the moon and the nearby plum tree.

'What's going on?' he mumbled, completely bewildered. Then he heard the cry of an animal: '*Miaoow.*'

'A sea cat? It can't be.' The house was some distance from the coast and he had never seen a black-tailed gull here before. Searching for the source of the sound, he saw a kitten, a grey tabby with white patches, sitting under the plum tree. It looked directly at Yoshio and mewed.

‘Mimi?’ The name came naturally to Yoshio’s lips. It was what he and Setsu had called the tiny, soaking-wet creature they had found mewing outside their front door on the night of a typhoon.

‘Poor little thing,’ Setsu had said, cradling it in her arms. From that moment on, the cat had become part of the Kurata family. They named her Mimi, meaning ‘ears’, because her ears were so big, and Setsu loved her like a child.

Cats’ lives are short, however, and in what seemed like no time at all, Mimi grew old and died. That was six months before Setsu’s illness was diagnosed, yet here the cat was.

And that wasn’t all. Suddenly, from right beside Yoshio came a voice he knew better than his own.

‘My darling.’

Sitting there next to him on the veranda was Setsu. She looked exactly as she had before her illness. Her hair was grey but there was colour in her plump cheeks. *So my wish has been granted*, Yoshio thought, shocked: *Setsu has come to lead me into the next world.*

Setsu shook her head. ‘No, that’s not why I’m here.’ She seemed to know what he was thinking. ‘Don’t get ahead of yourself, now. You still have some time left.’

'Oh . . .' Yoshio's shoulders slumped, but he told himself firmly that Setsu was there at that moment, and that was enough. There was something he needed to tell her.

If there is a life after death, Setsu, I want you to be my wife there too. He had tried to say this to her many times as she lay in her hospital bed, but something had always stopped him.

He and Setsu had not been able to have children. When they consulted a doctor, Yoshio was told that an illness he had contracted as a child had left him infertile. And while he had not minded for himself, whenever he saw his wife smiling at a child in the park or at the supermarket, or flicking through leaflets for children's clothes that came inside the newspaper, his heart sank. Lying in the dark at night, sometimes he wondered if it would have been better if they'd never met.

He wanted to be with Setsu in the next life, but not if it would rob her of the chance of having children all over again. He couldn't bear the thought of making her unhappy.

Yoshio hung his head. He could not look at his wife, could not bring himself to ask what he wanted to ask. As he stared at the ground, he noticed that the mist seemed to be clearing. Perhaps Setsu would soon slip away, fed up with his spinelessness.

The mew of a cat broke the silence. '*Miaow.*'

It was the sound Mimi had made whenever someone new came to the house. Memories of those times immediately flooded back into Yoshio's mind. And then he heard a woman's voice. It belonged to neither Setsu nor Kotoko.

Please, eat while it's still warm.

Yoshio gave a start. There could be no doubt about it – it was the voice of Nanami, Kai's late mother, coming from beyond the mist, which swirled and thickened once again. He squinted into the haze, trying to make her out.

Go on, it'll get cold, she urged.

Yoshio recalled what people had told him about the magic of the Chibineko Kitchen. Sometimes the dead appeared to you – but they could only stay while the kagezen was steaming hot. He knew his time with Setsu was short and he didn't want to be left with regrets, but still he hesitated.

Nanami's voice came to him again: *I think, perhaps, your wife is waiting for you to speak.*

He looked up tentatively and saw that it was true. Setsu was smiling at him. There was no disappointment in her face, only tenderness.

Yoshio took a breath and said, 'Setsu – be with me in the next world.'

It was his second time proposing to Setsu: he had fallen in love with her as a young man and he loved her still, at the very end of his life.

A heavy silence hung in the air, then Setsu spoke. 'Why on earth would you ask that now?' Her voice was gentle, but it contained a note of rebuke. 'We made a promise when we married. You and I are husband and wife – in this world and the next.'

'So, you're saying . . .'

'Of course,' Setsu nodded, 'and there's something I want to say to you too. Thank you – for the days we spent together; for all the laughter we had in our lives.'

Happy tears welled in Yoshio's eyes. He wanted to reply, but couldn't find the words.

And then, all of a sudden, Setsu was gone. Her bowl of pickled-plum rice porridge was cold and Yoshio was alone. He put a hand to his cheek. He was sure he'd been crying yet his face was dry. Looking out at the garden, he saw that the mist had cleared and that Mimi was gone. Instead, Kai and Kotoko stood beside him.

'Some hot tea for you.'

Kai had brewed some hojicha. The fragrance of the roasted green tea leaves drifted through the air. Yoshio watched the steam rising from the teacup. It was as though nothing had happened. There was no imprint in the cushion next to him on which Setsu had sat. *Was I dreaming?*

Yoshio was puzzling over this when Kotoko draped a blanket over his shoulders. 'You'll get cold,' she said timidly.

He thanked her and then heard a faint voice.

Aren't you lucky, love, to have the young ones looking after you so well?

But when he looked around, Setsu was nowhere to be seen. He wondered if he had only imagined it, and then she spoke again.

If it is just a dream – does that matter?

Perhaps she was right. For the first time since Setsu's death, Yoshio felt content. He didn't know how long he had left – days, weeks, perhaps months. Yet he no longer felt he wanted to die. Setsu had loved this life, so he would etch the events of each day he had left into his mind and make a gift of them to his wife in the world beyond. Words did not always come easily to Yoshio but he was certain Setsu would listen, and that there would be plenty of time for talking.

*

Yoshio needed to find a way to thank Kai and Kotoko. It was all due to them that he could now live out his last days without regret.

'I want you to have the plums Setsu pickled,' he said. 'Take them back with you to the Chibineko Kitchen.'

'But they must be very precious to you . . .' Kai hesitated. He had always been a reserved, kind boy. Yoshio remembered how he had stayed at home to help his mother with the restaurant instead of going off to university, and when Nanami was hospitalised, her son had visited her every day. Her death must have come as a terrible shock. But there was not much an old man like Yoshio could do to comfort Kai.

'I'll be going back into hospital tomorrow, and this house won't be here much longer,' Yoshio said. 'If you leave the plums here, they'll only go to waste.'

'Why not take them to the hospital with you?' Having spent so much time there, Kai knew that patients on the palliative care ward could eat what they liked.

But Yoshio had no need of the plums now. Setsu would not appear to him a second time. 'No, you two should have them,' he insisted. He felt that Setsu would like them to go to the young folk.

'Then we'll gladly take them,' Kai said, and Kotoko hastily bowed her head. 'Thank you.'

Yoshio was relieved to have found a home for the jar of pickled plums.

You old softie. You're acting as if you're marrying off one of your children. The words found their way to Yoshio and his mind was filled with an image of Setsu, smiling at him. He couldn't help but smile too as he gazed out into the dark night.

A special recipe from the Chibineko Kitchen

Umebishio: Pickled-plum jam

Ingredients

- Approx. 8 pickled plums
- Cooking saké – to taste
- Sugar – to taste

Method

1. Soak the pickled plums in water overnight to remove the salt.
2. Remove the stones from the fruit. Chop the plums very finely with a kitchen knife and then press them through a sieve.
3. Heat the plum paste in a saucepan and add saké and sugar to taste. Stir until glossy and well combined, taking care that the jam doesn't burn.

Tips

Mirin can be used instead of saké; but it's sweeter, so you may want to reduce the amount of sugar accordingly. You can also replace the sugar with an alternative sweetener or sugar syrup.

4

A little kitten and a meal for the restaurant staff

かずさ和牛

Kazusa wagyu

A popular brand of Japanese beef, local to Chiba Prefecture, that is marbled and yet light in flavour. The fat has a low melting point, meaning the beef almost melts in the mouth.

At Kazusa Wagyu Kobo deli and restaurant in Kimitsu, you can try this beef in classic dishes such as croquettes, beef katsu and hamburgers, as well as sukiyaki, steak, and seared wagyu nigiri sushi.

NB Kazusa wagyu is not the prefecture's only connection with cattle farming. Chiba is also said to be the birthplace of Japan's dairy industry. In the 1700s, the shogun Tokugawa Yoshimune imported Indian white cattle and reared them on the Mineokamaki pastures on the south of the Boso Peninsula. He used the milk to make hakugyuraku, a product similar to butter.

In Kai's hand was a notebook. Along with recipes, it contained details about the restaurant's regular customers. Kotoko's brother and Yoshio Kurata were in there, though it wasn't Kai who had written their names, but his mother. She had begun keeping the notebook when she first opened the Chibineko Kitchen. In spare moments during her working day and after closing time, she would sit at a table in the restaurant and jot down her notes. She never neglected this task no matter how tired she might be. Kai had once told her she should give herself a break first, after the last diners had left, but she shook her head. 'It wouldn't do to forget.'

Nanami had been putting things down on paper for her son's sake, and she gave him the notebook when she found out that she was ill. Her instructions were easy to follow and they allowed Kai to take over the running of the restaurant seamlessly – everything he needed to know was written in the book.

'Look after the place for me until I'm better,' his mother said to him just before she went into hospital. 'I'll be back soon.'

Kai nodded but didn't respond. Nanami had been told that her cancer was inoperable. She wasn't going in for treatment, she was entering palliative care – but she spoke as though she were just popping out to the supermarket.

Next Nanami turned to the kitten. 'Chibi, you be good too.'

'*Miaow*,' he mewed in response, and seemed to nod. Cats were mysterious creatures – sometimes you couldn't help but believe they understood you.

'And look after Kai,' Nanami added.

'*Miaow*.' Chibi's expression was almost serious. *Leave it to me*, he seemed to be saying.

Nanami had spoken in jest, but she must have been concerned for her son too. He had caused her more worry than the average child.

Twenty-four years earlier, Kai had been born prematurely. His health was poor and the doctors had told Kai's mother and father that he might not reach adulthood.

His parents were desperate to see their son grow up happy and healthy. As well as rushing him into hospital whenever he was ill, they petitioned the gods on his behalf. They prayed at shrines and at temples, and every time there was a saucer moon, they would make a wish on that too.

Their prayers were answered. As Kai grew up, his health gradually improved until eventually he rarely even caught colds.

But then Nanami's husband went missing at sea. Kai felt as though he had been given his own health in exchange for his father.

After the loss of her husband, Kai's mother opened the Chibineko Kitchen. 'At first I thought of naming it the Sea Cat Diner, after the black-tailed gulls, but there are plenty of other restaurants with names like that,' Nanami said. 'We don't want people getting confused.'

As it happened, the pet cat they had been keeping when they first opened the restaurant died of old age when Kai was in junior high school: one day, all of a sudden, it just stopped moving. For a while after that they were without a cat, but then about six months before Kai's mother went into hospital, a second Chibi joined the family. Nanami had found him abandoned by the seashore and brought him home.

'We're called the Chibineko Kitchen after all, so we've got to have a cat,' she said, stroking the kitten's head as he purred.

The restaurant was doing well enough that they could afford to keep Chibi, all thanks to the mysterious kagezen, but neither Kai nor his mother had ever seen the dead themselves, or heard their voices. Kai had prepared remembrance meals many times, in the hope of seeing his father and then later his mother, but they never appeared.

Now that his mother was dead, there was nothing to keep Kai here. He had given up on his father long ago. *It's time to leave this place. I'll take Chibi and go travelling,* he decided, making plans to go once the customary forty-nine days of mourning had elapsed. After his mother's funeral, he erased the lettering on the chalkboard outside the restaurant.

The Chibineko Kitchen
We serve remembrance meals.

He hesitated for a moment and then wiped away the drawing of the kitten too. It disappeared cleanly, without leaving a trace. It was his mother who had originally written the words and drawn the picture, but whenever the chalk lines grew faint, Kai had gone over them again, until they were as much in his writing as in hers.

This chalkboard wouldn't be needed any longer; Kai planned to sell it off along with the restaurant. He hung a sign on the door saying, 'Closed: No Longer in Business', and then there was nothing more to do. He rarely watched television or spent time online even before his mother's death, and he had no real friends who he wanted to see at a time like this – though there was one person, but she was a customer, rather than a friend. And besides, he had already informed her of the restaurant's closure.

Kai couldn't break the habit of waking before dawn even though he was no longer opening the restaurant every morning. When his mother was alive the Chibineko Kitchen had served breakfast, lunch and dinner. It was Kai who had started closing early in order that he could visit Nanami in hospital in the afternoons; he had wanted to spend as much time with her as he could. At first he had considered only opening the restaurant in the evenings but then he remembered what his mother had said about breakfast: *The morning meal is very important. It marks the beginning of a new day for each of our customers.* As the nearby steelworks operated night shifts, there were those who came to eat on their way home from work.

But all that was over now.

'It's about time for some breakfast,' Kai said to himself that morning, referring not to his own meal but to the cat's. Chibi slept in Nanami's room these days, seeming to take comfort from being among her belongings and her familiar scent. Sometimes Chibi would knead at her blanket with his paws, something Kai knew that kittens did when missing their own mothers. But every morning without fail, the little cat would wake up at dawn and come down to the restaurant for his breakfast. It was what he had always done, ever since he joined the family.

Kai lay in bed aimlessly as eight o'clock came and went. At last he dragged himself up and went downstairs. The shutters were lowered, the room was dark and it was silent except for the ticking of the old grandfather clock. Ordinarily Chibi would be twining himself around Kai's legs by now, but Kai hadn't heard a single mew.

That's strange. He turned on the lights, looked over by the clock and under the tables, but still there was no sign of the cat.

'Chibi?' Total silence. Kai went back upstairs and searched all over the house but the kitten was nowhere to be found.

Had he got outside again? Chibi had a penchant for escape and seemed to be always finding openings just big enough to slip through. Given that he didn't normally go further than the chalkboard outside the door, Kai had never worried about him getting lost or being hit by a car, but now they were moving away, he would have to keep a much closer eye on the little cat.

Kai went down to the restaurant again and opened the door. The sun had risen over the seaside town and the sky was blue as far as the eye could see. The view looked just as it always had.

The chalkboard, with all the writing erased, was still standing by the door but there was no sign of Chibi. Maybe he'd been watching the gulls and, full of curiosity, had gone chasing after them. Too late, Kai regretted letting the kitten have the run of the place. His father was gone, his mother had passed away and now even Chibi had disappeared, leaving him all alone. Feeling a deep sense of unease, he rushed out onto the seashell path calling for the little cat, afraid that he might never see him again. And then . . .

'*Miaow*,' came the response from a little way off.

Kai stopped still and listened and then he heard footsteps. Someone was coming towards him. Chibi's mewing grew closer and then Kotoko appeared, the kitten in her arms.

'Hello. I'm back again.'

'But why?' Kai asked, bewildered. Kotoko knew he was closing the restaurant.

'I came to make breakfast,' she replied, looking directly at Kai. 'Please will you let me cook for you?'

It feels as though I'm proposing to him, Kotoko thought. Her cheeks burned but she held her nerve. She'd come such a long way, after all.

The last time Kotoko had visited the Chibineko Kitchen was the night they cooked peanut rice for Yoshio Kurata, but she had also travelled out to Chiba yesterday to visit the old man in hospital. When she found him, he was eating shaved ice topped with strawberry syrup – something that was easy for the patients on the palliative care ward to manage. Between small spoonfuls, Yoshio talked to Kotoko about Kai: he was worried about how the young man was faring since his mother's death.

'It's hard losing your family. He'll need your shoulder to lean on,' he told her. He seemed to be under the impression that Kotoko and Kai were romantically involved. She wanted to correct him but Yoshio wasn't listening. He kept talking, almost to himself. 'They were always good to me at the Chibineko Kitchen. I used to go there after closing time, sometimes . . .'

He told Kotoko how he had stopped at the restaurant on his way home from visiting Setsu in hospital one day, only to find it was shut. He was about to turn round when he heard the clink of the doorbell and Nanami emerged. She must have noticed him standing outside.

'Come in,' she said, ushering the hesitant Yoshio into the restaurant.

'I'm afraid this is all we've got left,' Nanami apologised as she served Yoshio's meal. It was the food intended for the restaurant staff – Nanami was treating Yoshio to the dish she would normally have shared with her son.

'Good meal, that was . . .' Yoshio mumbled. And suddenly Kotoko had an idea: she would cook that same dish for Kai. She didn't know how well she'd be able to make it and she worried that Kai might think she was intruding, but he had saved her and she wanted to return the favour. He was hurting and the least she could do was try to help.

Inside the restaurant, Kai fed Chibi and he and Kotoko drank some tea. Neither of them spoke for some time. Then, when Chibi went to curl up on the rocking chair, Kotoko stood up.

'I'll go and buy the ingredients now,' she announced. She must have been waiting for the shops to open for the day.

'Shall I come with you?'

Kotoko shook her head. 'I'll be all right on my own.'

Kai sat in the empty restaurant, torn between wishing Kotoko would leave him alone and wanting to know what she would make him. When Kotoko had cooked for Yoshio, the old man had said that his late wife appeared to him. Would her cooking make the dead appear to Kai too? Would he see his mother?

Kai had never really believed what the restaurant's customers told him about the kagezen. He thought it was far more likely that the food simply stimulated their memories, so that they imagined they saw their loved ones. The dead who appeared only ever seemed to say things that suited the living. But even a waking dream would be enough for Kai. He wanted to see his mother, to talk to her just one more time before he left the town behind.

'Don't you agree?' he said to Chibi.

From the rocking chair Chibi made a yawn-like noise. He didn't seem particularly interested.

'You don't think I'm correct?' he asked the kitten, slightly annoyed. And then the doorbell clinked and Kotoko was back.

Kai offered her the use of the restaurant kitchen, which was still connected to the gas, electricity and water.

'Are you sure you don't mind?' she asked.

'Of course. This is no longer a restaurant anyway.'

Kotoko hesitated for a moment before setting her bag down on a chair by the wall and going into the kitchen.

Half an hour later, she returned. She was carrying a cast-iron pot and a portable hob; it looked as though she intended to cook at the table. She also brought out some sliced long green onions and beef.

'It's Kazusa wagyu,' she said. Kai knew the type of beef, and judging by the pot and the ingredients, he could guess what Kotoko was planning to make. Nonetheless he asked her, just to be sure.

'Sukiyaki,' Kotoko replied, as expected. 'It won't take long.' She made the sauce first, mixing soy sauce with cooking saké, sugar and water in a pan over the heat. Then she melted beef fat in the cast-iron pot and fried the long green onions until they were lightly browned. Finally, with the cast-iron pot still on the hob, she added the sukiyaki sauce and beef.

'You're making it Kanto-style,' Kai commented, noticing that she cooked the beef in the sauce straight away, rather than frying it in beef fat first as was traditional in the Kansai region. Kai had never tried Kansai-style sukiyaki, but he assumed it must taste similar to yakiniku – meat barbecued on a grill.

'Yes. This is the way we cook it at home,' said Kotoko. *Just like in my family*, Kai thought.

As they spoke, the sukiyaki simmered away and the air filled with the aroma of sweetened soy sauce.

Chibi twitched his nose and looked up at Kotoko. '*Miaow*.' It was as though he was letting her know it was ready. Kotoko seemed to agree.

'Yes, it's just about there,' she said, cracking an egg into a small bowl and serving up some of the beef into another. 'Here you are.'

'Thank you,' Kai said, taking the bowl Kotoko handed him. Chibi had been right, the meat was done to perfection. It was still a little pink – Kazusa wagyu was best when you didn't cook it for too long.

'Itadakimasu.' Kai bowed his head to Kotoko, picked up a piece of beef in his chopsticks, dipped it into the raw egg and put it in his mouth. The Kazusa wagyu was sweet, juicy, and so tender it seemed to dissolve on his tongue. The silky egg yolk brought out the flavour of the beef perfectly.

The dish was delicious; it held its own against any sukiyaki Kai had eaten before, and it reminded him of the sukiyaki his mother used to make for their customers, but Kai knew this wasn't it. This wasn't his remembrance meal. Sukiyaki was a popular order at the Chibineko Kitchen, but Kai and his mother had never eaten it at their own table. It brought back no memories of her.

'I'm very sorry Ms Niki, but—'

Kai was about to put down his chopsticks, disappointed, when Kotoko interrupted.

'And now let me finish preparing your meal.'

Kai was confused. He was already eating – what could she mean?

Kotoko scooped some rice into a large bowl and ladled some of the sukiyaki over the top. It had continued to simmer away in the warm cast-iron pot, and the beef was now cooked through, the long green onions soft and falling apart.

'Sukiyaki-don,' Kotoko said, holding the bowl out to Kai.

He said nothing. He could only gaze at the food as memories of eating sukiyaki-don with his mother filled his mind.

The meals that a restaurant provides for its staff are called 'makanai'. Though the Chibineko Kitchen was a family business and didn't employ anyone else, they still ate a kind of makanai every night after the restaurant closed. Sukiyaki-don was one such meal.

A lot of the customers ordered sukiyaki so Nanami made sure they were always well-stocked with the ingredients. Then, after closing time, she would ladle the leftovers onto rice for Kai, serving it this way to make the small amount of meat go further. After dishing out portions for herself and her son, Nanami would set out a tray for Kai's father. She and Kai would sit side by side at one of the restaurant tables with the kagezen opposite them, and they would eat together as a family. It was a time in which to slow down and take a breath at the end of each day.

'Um . . .' Kotoko looked embarrassed, breaking into Kai's reverie, the bowl of sukiyaki-don still in her hands.

'I'm sorry. My mind was elsewhere,' Kai said and took the warm, heavy bowl from her.

'Itadakimasu,' he said once again, and picked up a piece of long green onion with his chopsticks. The slow cooking had made it translucent and so soft it looked ready to fall to pieces even before reaching his mouth.

His stomach rumbled. He hadn't had much of an appetite since his mother died but now, suddenly, he was hungry. Kotoko had put out red chilli powder on the table but Kai wanted to taste the dish just as it was. As he bit into the piece of onion, its sweet, tangy flavour burst over his tongue, all the deliciousness of sukiyaki condensed in a single mouthful. The familiar taste drew Kai into the past once more, bringing back memories of his mother's death – memories filled with sorrow.

'Thank you for looking after her,' Kai said to the doctors and nurses who had taken care of Nanami until the end. They bowed to him and then left the room, giving Kai time alone with his mother. He looked down at her face. Her expression was peaceful and there was no sign of the cancer that had ravaged her body – she could have been asleep. Kai almost felt that if he called out to her, she would open her eyes. Instead, he touched her cheek. It was already growing cold. And of course, her eyes stayed closed.

Kai thought of the days that had led up to this one. There was the time his mother had handed him her glasses.

'I'm not using these at the moment,' she had said.

Nanami was a keen reader, and even in hospital she had read non-stop, right until she became unable to raise herself up in bed. She was on an IV drip and could no longer eat properly, let alone read. It must have been hard for her, yet her voice was light when she asked Kai: 'Will you keep my glasses safe for me? When I get better and come home, I'll want to do lots of reading.'

Kai knew that, really, she was giving him her glasses as a keepsake; Nanami was preparing for her death. The thought brought him close to tears but he forced a note of cheerfulness into his voice.

'May I use them until you come back?' He didn't need glasses himself, but he would get the lenses changed so he could wear them. He wanted to feel her close to him.

'All right, but don't break them.' His mother smiled, but through the oxygen mask her voice was hoarse and so quiet he could barely make it out.

Kai hoped for a miracle. He wanted to believe, and sometimes really did, that his mother would get better – that there would be a day when she returned home and they lived together again. But Nanami never recovered. When she finally came home, it was as a corpse.

Chibi had stayed at the Chibineko Kitchen while Kai and Nanami were away. Now, he looked at the lifeless face of Kai's mother and mewed, as though trying to talk to her. When she didn't reply, the little cat tilted his head in puzzlement.

'She's dead, Chibi.' Tears spilled from Kai's eyes and he felt a great weight pressing on his chest. But he had no time for crying. There were funeral arrangements to be made. He organised a Buddhist priest to read a sutra for his mother and then he had her body cremated. Kai had wanted to say goodbye to Nanami with Chibi by his side, but he couldn't take the kitten to the crematorium. So he carried out the funeral rites alone, picking his mother's bones out of the ashes with chopsticks and placing them in an urn along with her glasses, to which he had returned his mother's old lenses.

He put his hands together. Though Kai had never really believed in an afterlife, nevertheless he offered a prayer for his mother in the next world. *I hope you have everything you need, and all the books your heart desires. I hope you are free of troubles, in that place where there is no sickness.*

Kai finished his bowl of sukiyaki-don, savouring the last morsels of rice drenched in sauce.

'Delicious,' he said, putting his bowl and chopsticks down. The meal was over. He saw that Kotoko had set out a portion of sukiyaki-don for his mother at the place opposite him, but it was getting cold, the steam dwindling away.

Kai had certainly thought of his mother as he ate the remembrance meal, but she hadn't appeared in the restaurant or spoken to him. *So, there will be no miracle for me after all.*

Kotoko looked at him inquiringly. With a heavy heart Kai was about to tell her that nothing had happened, when Chibi began to mew sweetly, as though speaking to someone. The little kitten had gone over to the chair on which Kotoko had left her things, jumped up onto it and begun to nose at her bag.

'*Miaow,*' he mewed again.

Except this time the noise sounded muffled.

'What's wrong?' Kai asked Chibi, concerned. But to his surprise, his own voice was also muted. And stranger still, Kotoko's bag had begun to emit a dazzling light which radiated outwards, enveloping Kai completely. At the same time, he could see a thick mist spreading through the restaurant.

'What on earth . . .?' Kai turned to find Kotoko had vanished even though she had been there only moments before. And then he heard the door of the Chibineko Kitchen open.

Clink, clink. Someone stepped inside. It was hard to be certain in the bright light and the mist, but Kai thought he could make out the silhouette of a woman. *It can't be,* he thought, just as Chibi gave an affectionate little mew and darted towards the figure at the door. As the woman's face came into focus, Kai saw that she was wearing the glasses he himself had used until just recently.

'Mother . . .' She had come home.

Chibi rubbed himself against her legs.

'You've been a good kitten, haven't you?' Nanami said, looking down at him.

'*Miaow,*' Chibi replied proudly. Nanami stroked his head and, apparently satisfied, the kitten returned to the rocking chair.

Kai's mother sat down opposite her son at the table and watched the wisps of steam rising from the food in front of her.

'There's something you wanted to speak to me about, isn't there?' she said.

'Yes . . .' Everything he'd been told about the kagezen was true which meant he mustn't waste any time: the steam from the sukiyaki-don was already petering out. 'I'm closing the Chibineko Kitchen,' he said simply.

'Ah yes, you're going to leave this town.' Nanami already seemed to know of his plans.

'I'm sorry,' Kai said, bowing his head. He knew how important the restaurant had been to his mother, and he felt terrible about closing it permanently.

But Nanami wasn't angry. 'You don't need to apologise. But please look after yourself on your travels.'

When Kai had been ill as a child, she had stayed up all night to nurse him, never leaving his side. She had even carried him on her back to the hospital several times. Kai remembered now how the warmth of her body felt. *I never repaid her for everything she did for me*, he thought, and wanted to cry, but he couldn't have his mother worrying about him when she went back to the next world.

Nanami saw him fighting back the tears and said tenderly, 'It's all right to let it out. Everyone needs a place where they can cry.'

She went on, as though reciting a story: 'Whenever life gets difficult or painful, even after you've moved away, you can always come back here and cry. This is the town where you were born, the town where you lived with me and your father. This is your home, whether the restaurant is open or not.'

'Mother . . .'

'What is it?' said Nanami, but Kai couldn't go on. As he cried, his mother reached out and stroked his head, comforting him just as she had when he was a child. Then, when he was a little calmer, she stood up.

'It's time for me to go now.'

Kai looked at the table and saw that the sukiyaki-don was no longer steaming. He had known that the moment couldn't last, yet he didn't want to part from her; he didn't want to be left all alone – alone except for Chibi, of course.

'Mother, please don't go,' he begged.

'Now, you know it doesn't work like that,' his mother said ruefully, looking towards the door. 'Ah, here he is to accompany me back,' she murmured.

'What?' Kai said, and then he heard the restaurant door open. Turning round, he saw a tall figure standing in the doorway, haloed in the light and mist. The man's features were a lot like his own and Kai knew exactly who it was, even though it had been twenty years.

'Father . . .' The word left his lips before he even had time to think. The man nodded in acknowledgement.

Kai wanted to rush over to the door but his body wouldn't move – it was as though he was paralysed.

'I'm sorry, Kai. It looks as though only one of us is allowed to speak with you,' Nanami explained. Kai wondered whether his father was bending the rules by being here at all. Perhaps he had had to press his case with the gods before they would let him come as far as the door.

Nanami walked to her husband's side. Both parents looked at their son. The true moment of parting had come. Kai steeled himself – he had something important to say.

'Father, mother. I was so happy having you as my parents. I'm still happy now.'

His parents smiled across the room at him, and then his mother spoke her final words. 'We were so glad we had you too, Kai. Goodbye, now.'

With that, they were gone. The doorbell clinked and the morning mist cleared.

Kotoko had been watching Kai as the minutes passed. He had finished the sukiyaki-don and then gone completely still.

She ventured a tiny sound but he didn't seem to hear her.

Had his mother appeared to him? Kotoko looked round the restaurant. When her brother had visited her here a bright mist had filled the room and the pendulum of the old clock had stopped, but there was no sign of anything out of the ordinary happening now. Chibi was still curled up on the rocking chair, dreaming, perhaps, and mewing now and then as though talking in his sleep.

No miracle after all, then?

Kai was experiencing something strange, Kotoko was sure of it, though she had no way of knowing what, so she just remained silent and watched him. Time crept on and the sukiyaki-don cooled. Suddenly Kai's gaze shifted to the doorway.

'. . . So happy . . .' she thought she heard him mumble, but she couldn't be sure. Tears were pouring down his cheeks but his face was composed.

Kotoko set a cup of green tea down on the table in front of him. 'Here you go,' she said, and this time Kai looked up. She saw that his tears had vanished, though surely he hadn't had time to wipe them away. He took a sip of the tea and then put the cup down.

'Thank you for the food.'

The meal was over and there was no further reason for her to stay. But she had one last thing to give him before leaving. Kotoko fetched her belongings from the chair and took out a paper bag with a ribbon stuck onto it. 'Here,' she said in a tiny mouse-like voice.

Kai looked surprised. 'For me?'

Kotoko nodded and blushed. She had never given a present to a man outside her family before, and her embarrassment made her hands tremble as she held it out to him. 'Will you take it?' she asked, the question coming out as a squeak.

What if he says no? she thought, avoiding his gaze and fighting the urge to flee the restaurant.

But Kai didn't refuse. He took the gift from Kotoko. 'Thank you very much. May I open it?'

'Y . . . Yes, of course.'

'A pair of glasses!' Kai said, when he had slid them out of the paper bag. Kotoko had chosen a pair almost identical to the ones he had been wearing when she first met him – which had belonged to Kai's mother, as Yoshio had told her at the hospital. Perhaps it was too forward of her to give him such a personal gift but Kai didn't seem angry.

'So that explains the light . . .' he murmured enigmatically.

'What do you mean?' Kotoko asked, but Kai didn't explain.

'Nothing – I'm just talking to myself.' He gave a little shake of his head, then put on the glasses and turned to Kotoko. 'A perfect fit.' He beamed at her. The glasses suited him well and so did the smile.

The tension lifted from Kotoko's body. She had done what she had set out to do. Now all that remained was to get back on the train and go home. Kotoko had her own life and Kai had his, but something about this simple fact made her terribly sad. She wanted to invite him to see her play, but he'd only just lost his mother, and he'd be leaving town soon. She didn't have the courage to broach the subject.

'Well—' she began, about to say her goodbyes and go when Chibi interrupted.

'*Miaow.*' The kitten had woken from his nap and had fixed his eyes on Kai.

'Yes, you're right,' Kai addressed Chibi, as though he had understood his mew. He turned back to Kotoko, his usual courteous self. 'You've already cooked for me and given me these glasses so I hesitate to ask, but I wonder if you might do one more favour for me?'

Kotoko nodded. 'Y . . . Yes, all right. If there's something I can help with.'

Chibi swished his tail from side to side and, though she wasn't sure, she thought he seemed pleased.

There was a note of relief in Kai's voice too. 'I very much appreciate it. Well then . . .' He stood up and headed for the door. Chibi followed, curling the tip of his tail. Kotoko watched them go, failing to understand what she was supposed to do until Chibi looked back and mewed. *Come on!* he seemed to be saying, so Kotoko hurried after the pair. When she reached the door, Kai held it open for her like a doorman at a grand hotel.

The doorbell clinked as the brisk November wind came rushing in; it felt pleasant on Kotoko's face. The beautiful Uchibo coast stretched out ahead of her. There was the beach where she'd first met Kai and the path strewn with white seashells. The sound of the waves mingled with the cries of the black-tailed gulls. The sky was an endless blue.

Kotoko looked at Kai, who had crouched down in front of the chalkboard by the door. All the writing had been rubbed off, along with the drawing of the kitten.

Chibi sat daintily beside Kai, twitching his tail and ears and mewing as though encouraging him.

'*Miaow.*'

'Yes. That's the plan,' Kai replied. He picked up a piece of chalk and began to write.

The Chibineko Kitchen
We serve remembrance meals.

The letters flowing from Kai's hand reminded Kotoko of white clouds floating in a blue sky. They were free – different from the lettering that had been there before. This must be Kai's own handwriting.

'*Miaow?*' Chibi mewed, as if to say, *Haven't you forgotten something?*

Kai laughed. 'All right, all right.' The chalk danced across the board spelling out one more sentence.

This restaurant has a cat.

'*Miaow.*' Chibi looked proudly at these words, which Kai had written out larger than previously, and mewed, satisfied.

Kai chuckled, and then he said to Kotoko, 'I've decided not to close up after all.'

'R . . . Really?'

'Yes. I'm going to continue running the Chibineko Kitchen.'

'I'm so glad!' Relief washed over her.

'Will you come and eat here again?' Kai asked.

'Of course!' Kotoko could hear the lightness in her own voice. She would get to taste Kai's cooking again. She would get to see him again.

As she stood there, filled with emotion, Kai said, 'Now, the request I wanted to make of you . . .'

Kotoko had almost forgotten. 'What is it?' she asked nervously, unable to guess. Kai held out the chalk.

'Would you draw a picture of Chibi on the board?'

'What? I . . . I can't!' Kotoko shook her head. There was no way a drawing of hers would be worthy of the chalkboard which served as the restaurant's official sign. But Kai and Chibi wouldn't back down.

'*Miaow.*'

'Please?'

They could plead all they liked, but Kotoko couldn't do it and that was that. Flustered, she was considering running away when Kai said earnestly, 'I would like . . . I want you to be the one to draw the picture, Kotoko.'

Kotoko. Kai had called her by her given name for the first time. She blushed and lowered her head to hide her red cheeks.

'I . . . Sorry,' Kai apologised, panicking.

'*Miaow.*' Even Chibi seemed contrite, his back arched.

Kotoko couldn't help but laugh. Whenever she came to this restaurant, she left it smiling.

Chibi looked at her, puzzled.

'Kotoko?' Kai spoke her name again, his voice confused but warm, and Kotoko felt herself relax. It was time to stop holding back. She had never drawn a cat before, but she decided to give it a go; even if it was terrible, she would treasure the memory.

'The chalk, please,' she said decisively.

'Right – yes,' Kai said, passing it to her. Chibi pricked up his ears, his funny little face expectant.

'It might not be very good, so don't laugh, OK?' Kotoko warned the pair of them with a smile, and then she set the chalk racing across the board. She could sense that today would be different from all the days that had come before. This was the beginning of something new.

A special recipe from the Chibineko Kitchen

Sukiyaki-don: Beef hotpot, served over rice

Ingredients (serves 4)

- 400g beef, thinly sliced (sukiyaki beef is best, if available)
- 2 long green onions (naganegi) cut in diagonal slices. (You can substitute these with spring onions or baby leeks.)
- 100ml each of soy sauce, cooking saké and water
- Sugar – a little
- Beef fat – a little
- 4 bowls of rice, freshly cooked

Method

1. In a small saucepan, combine the soy sauce, saké, sugar and water to make the sukiyaki sauce. Heat gently until the sugar has dissolved.

2. Melt the beef fat in a cast-iron pot. Add the long green onions and fry until lightly browned.
3. Add the sukiyaki sauce and beef to the pot and bring to a simmer. When the ingredients are cooked to your liking, remove from the heat (a longer cooking time will make the onions sweeter).
4. Ladle the sukiyaki over the bowls of freshly cooked rice.

Tips

If you prefer a stronger flavour, use 150ml each of soy sauce and saké. However, note that the ingredients for sukiyaki-don are simmered for longer than for regular sukiyaki, so you may wish to season lightly to avoid the dish ending up too salty.